This book belongs to

_____

Once Upon A Princess

Volume One

Stories translated from the Disney Libri series by Carin McLain

Printed in Singapore

First Edition

1 2 3 4 5 6 7 8 9 10

Library of Congress Catalog Card Number: 2002110890

ISBN: 0-7868-3465-X

For more Disney Press fun, visit www.disneybooks.com

ONCE UPON A PRINCESS

VOLUME ONE

DISNEY PRESS

New York

TABLE OF CONTENTS

THE STORY OF
ARIEL

MONTH OF THE SHELL, FIRST DAY OF THE RED ALGAE

I'*ve decided that starting today I will keep a diary. I want to write down all the thoughts I can't share with anyone. I want to leave a record of my most secret adventures. Of course, I have to have secrets—because if my father ever knew about everything I do . . . Oh, Daddy is a good sea king, and I know he loves me. But he worries much too much about me! He always sends Sebastian along to keep an eye on me and make sure I don't have any fun. Oh, I know Sebastian is Daddy's most trusted adviser, and under that hard shell he's really sort of soft. But he sure can be crabby!*

Luckily, I can slip away from him once in a while to visit the surface. And I love writing all about the fantastic things I've seen up there. The human world is so fascinating!

Anyway, Daddy can never, ever know about any of this. He thinks I'm still a little girl, but he's wrong. I'm almost grown up, and the sea just isn't big enough for me anymore. I want to see the whole world. And that includes the human world above the sea. My most secret, exciting, wonderful dream? To meet a real, live human in person and talk to him. That would be the most incredible thing in the world!

I know what Daddy would say about that. He'd say that humans are all barbarians who kill sea creatures every chance they get. But I'm sure not all of them are like that. Daddy is very wise, but he doesn't know everything.

This evening, a little sea horse told me about a sunken ship he saw a few miles from the palace. Tomorrow, Flounder and I are going to check it out. I hope I find lots of interesting human objects to add to the collection in my secret hideaway! I'll just have to make sure I'm home in plenty of time for Daddy's concert. . . .

Oh! I'm so sleepy. Better get to bed now, or I'll be too tired to explore or sing tomorrow. Good night, Diary!

MERMAIDS, SHARKS, AND GUPPIES

"Ariel, wait for me!" Flounder, the little yellow fish gasped as he tried to keep up with the red-haired mermaid swimming ahead of him.

"Flounder, hurry up!" Ariel called, excitedly.

"You know I can't swim that fast!" Flounder cried.

Ariel waited impatiently for her best friend to catch up. "There it is," she said, pointing through the murky waters of the ocean floor at the ruins of a sunken ship ahead. "Isn't it fantastic?"

"Yeah, sure. It-it's great," Flounder stammered. But

he wasn't too sure about that. Being this far from the safety of the palace made him very, very nervous. There could be anything lurking in these deep, open waters. "Now let's get out of here," he added.

"You're not getting cold fins now, are you?" Ariel teased.

"Who, me? No way," Flounder answered, trying to cover up. "It's just that it looks damp in there, and I think I may be coming down with something," he said, suddenly starting to cough.

"All right, I'm going inside," Ariel said as she started swimming toward a porthole. "You just stay here and watch for sharks."

"What? Sharks!" Flounder exclaimed, hurrying after the little mermaid. "Ariel! Wait!"

"Flounder, don't be such a guppy," Ariel said, ignoring his worried comments as the two friends swam through the porthole.

"I am not a guppy!" Flounder cried, insulted. Then, pretending to be as brave and excited about the sunken ship as Ariel herself, he said, chuckling nervously, "This is great, I mean, I really, uh, love this excitement . . . adventure . . . danger lurking around every cor—AAAAAH!" His comment ended in a shriek of fear as he came across the skeleton of a sailor who had gone down with the ship.

Meanwhile, Ariel had already made her way up to a higher deck. She immediately spotted something shiny—a strange metal object with three prongs sticking out of some rotted wood.

"Oh, my gosh!" She exclaimed as she grabbed the item. "Have you ever seen anything so wonderful in your entire life?"

Flounder looked at the metal item curiously. "Wow, cool!" he agreed. "But, uh, what is it?"

"I don't know," Ariel replied, tucking the item into her sack. "But I bet Scuttle will!"

Scuttle was one of Ariel's surface friends. He was a seagull who knew all about the human world. He was always happy to look at the treasures the little mermaid found and tell her what they were (even if he didn't really know himself).

Flounder wasn't thinking about Scuttle just then. Was it his imagination, or had he just heard a deep, threatening rumble from outside the ship?

"What was that?" he asked nervously. "Did you hear something?"

But Ariel wasn't listening. She had just found another weird-looking human object. It was made out of wood, and it had a wide hole at one end and a smaller, flatter hole at the other. She picked it up and stared at it. "Hmm, I wonder what this one is?"

"Ariel!" Flounder was growing more nervous by the second.

Ariel glanced at him. "Flounder, will you relax?" she said. "Nothing is going to happen!"

At that moment, a huge, shadowy shape loomed up right behind the little yellow fish. Flounder screamed in terror. "Aaah! Shark!" he shrieked.

Flounder and Ariel swam for their lives. The giant shark came after them, smashing through the walls of the ship and tracking them around the mast. Finally, Ariel tricked it into swimming right into the metal hoop at the top of the ship's anchor. The shark was trapped!

"You big bully!" Flounder shouted. Then he and Ariel swam quickly away.

A few minutes later, they surfaced near a rocky

island. Scuttle was sunning himself there, but he came right over when he spotted them.

"Scuttle, look what we found!" Ariel exclaimed, holding up her bag.

"We were in this sunken ship, and it was really creepy," Flounder added.

"Human stuff, huh?" the seagull said knowingly. "Let me see."

He dug into the bag. The first thing he pulled out was the metal object.

"Look at this! Wow! This is special. This is very, very unusual," he said, examining the silver fork. "It's a dinglehopper! Humans use these little babies to straighten their hair out." He demonstrated, twisting the pointy parts of the item in the feathers on top of his head. "See? Just a little twirl here, and a yank there—" He finished with a flourish.

Ariel took back the item and stared at it in awe. "A dinglehopper!" she exclaimed.

"What about that one?" Flounder asked, pointing to the second item.

"Ah, this I haven't seen in years. This is wonder-ful—a banded bulbous snarfblatt," Scuttle announced, picking up the pipe. "Humans invented the snarfblatt to make fine music. Allow me—" He put the snarfblatt to his beak and blew, but all that came out was salt water and seaweed.

Meanwhile, Ariel's face had gone white. "Music!" She gasped. "Oh, the concert!" In all the excitement, it had completely slipped her mind! "Oh, my gosh, my father's going to kill me!" She grabbed her bag. "I'm sorry, I've got to go. Thank you, Scuttle!"

Ariel and Flounder swam back to the palace as fast as they could. But it was too late. The concert was over.

King Triton was very disappointed in his youngest daughter. "I just don't know what we're going to do with you, young lady," he thundered.

Ariel felt terrible. "I'm sorry. I just forgot!"

Triton shook his head. "As a result of your careless behavior—"

"Careless and reckless behavior!" Sebastian the crab interrupted furiously.

"The entire celebration was . . . eh . . ." Triton searched for the right word.

"Well it was ruined!" Sebastian shouted. "Completely destroyed! Thanks to you, I am the laughingstock of the entire kingdom!" Sebastian was the official court composer.

Flounder couldn't stand to hear anymore. "But it wasn't her fault!" he burst out. "First this shark chased us, and then this seagull came, and—"

"Seagull?" Triton repeated.

Flounder knew he'd just made a terrible mistake. He clapped his fins over his mouth, but it was too late. King Triton's face filled with anger.

"You went up to the surface again, didn't you?" he asked Ariel. "Didn't you?"

"Nothing happened!" Ariel protested.

"Oh, Ariel!" Triton grasped his forehead in frustration. "How many times must we go through this? You could have been seen by one of those barbarians, one of those humans!"

"Daddy, they're not barbarians," Ariel protested.

"They're dangerous!" Triton insisted. "Do you think I want to see my youngest daughter snared by some fish eater's hook?"

"I'm sixteen years old!" Ariel cried. "I'm not a child anymore!"

But King Triton would not back down. "As long as you live under *my* ocean, you'll obey *my* rules!" he shouted.

"But if you would just listen," Ariel tried to explain.

"Not another word!" the king yelled. "And I am never, never to hear of you going to the surface again. Is that clear?"

Ariel couldn't answer. She swam away in tears.

MONTH OF THE SHELL, THIRD DAY OF THE RED ALGAE

*I*t stinks being the youngest of seven sisters! Everyone thinks they can tell me what to do. Ever since I missed the concert, Daddy and my sisters keep acting like I kicked a pupfish or something. Oh, how I wish Flounder hadn't told about our visit to the surface. I've never seen Daddy so angry! If he had his way, he'd probably close me up in a clamshell to keep me safe. Or worse yet, he'll invite Talassio back for another visit to talk some sense into me.

Ha! I know Talassio is the son of Prince Cianos, Daddy's friend. And I know he means well. He's just so . . . so . . . boring! He's only eighteen years old—how can he already seem so dull? All he thinks about is finding a wife and settling down. My sisters think he's cute, and I guess they're right in a way. Talassio is tall and blond, with blue eyes and broad shoulders. But all he is to me is a cute young merman who's so boring, he'll put you to sleep.

Maybe he was trying to be serious just to impress me. Well, it didn't work. I told him that I was the youngest daughter, and according to our laws all my sisters have to get married before I can. You should've seen his face! I could just see him with gray hair and wrinkled scales, still waiting for his turn!

After he left, I felt a little guilty for telling a fib. But it was the only way I could get myself off the hook without hurting Talassio's feelings. I believe a little white lie is better than the truth sometimes, if it's for a good reason.

It's the same thing with Daddy, I think. Sometimes it's better that he not know everything I do or think or feel. For

example, right now I'm writing this in my secret hideaway, surrounded by my collection of things from the human world. Flounder is the only other one who knows about this place, but sometimes I wish I could bring Daddy here. Maybe if he could see all of the wonderful things I've collected, he would realize that humans can't be as terrible as he believes they are. Maybe he would start to understand just how much I long to know about the world up there above the surface. . . .

Hmm, I just heard a noise from outside. Could someone have stumbled onto my secret hiding place? Uh-oh—I'd better check! Until later, Diary . . .

THE STORM

"**S**ebastian!" Ariel cried as she spotted the crab tripping over a shiny hourglass in her secret hideaway.

"Ariel! What are you . . . How could you . . . er," Sebastian sputtered, gesturing around him with his claws. "What is all this?" The king had sent him to keep an eye on Ariel. And now that he'd followed her to this out-of-the-way cavern, he couldn't believe what he was seeing. Human objects! Dozens of them—maybe hundreds! King Triton would have a fit when he heard about it.

"It's just my collection," Ariel replied.

"Oh, I see, your collection," Sebastian said. "If your father knew about this place he'd—"

"You're not going to tell him, are you?" Flounder interrupted.

"Oh, please, Sebastian," Ariel added. "He would never understand!"

Well, she was right about that! Sebastian tried to be reasonable. "Come with me," he told her. "I'll take you home and get you something warm to drink."

At that moment, a shadow passed over the sun-filled entrance at the top of the grotto. Ariel looked up, ignoring Sebastian's words. "What do you suppose . . . ?" she began, already swimming upward.

She shot up quickly toward the surface, leaving Sebastian and Flounder behind. When she popped her head out of the water, she saw a ship.

The sight left her breathless. She had never seen a ship so close before! The humans on board seemed to be having a celebration. Multicolored sparks shot up into the sky, reflected on the calm surface of the water. Ariel could hear the sounds of happy music and festive voices coming from the deck.

Sebastian and Flounder popped up beside her. "Jumping jellyfish!" Sebastian exclaimed in shock when he saw the ship.

Ariel swam closer. Soon she was near enough to grab one of the rails of the deck and pull herself up for a better look. The sailors were too busy laughing, singing, and dancing to see her. But one creature did notice Ariel—a large, furry dog sniffed her out and came over to give her a friendly lick on the face. Barking wildly, he bounded over to one of the humans.

"Good boy, Max," the human greeted the dog fondly.

When Ariel took a good look at Max's master, she stared in amazement. The young man was tall, darkhaired, and incredibly handsome. She was sure he had to be the most beautiful human she had ever seen!

Just then, another human—an older man, with white hair—stepped forward and called for silence. "It is now my honor and privilege to present our esteemed Prince Eric with a very special, very expensive, very large birthday present." Smiling, he brought the handsome young man forward and gestured to a huge object covered by a cloth. "Happy birthday, Eric!" he cried, pulling off the fabric.

Ariel gasped. It was a life-size statue of the young man! Prince Eric, she thought, gazing at the human. It was a lovely name for such a beautiful person. She smiled as the prince thanked the older man, Grimsby, for the gift.

"Of course, I had hoped it would be a wedding present," Grimsby said. "The entire kingdom wants to see you happily settled down with the right girl."

"Oh, she's out there somewhere," Eric replied, perching on the edge of the deck and staring thoughtfully out to sea. "I just haven't found her yet."

"Uh, well, perhaps you haven't been looking hard enough," Grimsby suggested.

Eric chuckled. "Believe me, Grim, when I find her, I'll know. It'll just hit me—like lightning."

At that very moment, a bolt of lightning flashed through the night sky, and the rumble of thunder drowned out the men's voices.

"Hurricane!" one of the sailors cried. "Stand fast! Secure the rigging!"

A strong wind began to blow, thunder rattled, and rain pelted down on the deck. Soon the ship was tossing and turning in gigantic storm-blown waves.

Then a lightning bolt struck the mast—and the ship was in flames! It ran aground on some rocks and started to sink.

Ariel was safe because she could just go beneath the surface, but she was worried about the humans. She watched as they abandoned the ship, jumping into lifeboats. But Eric realized one member of the crew had been left behind.

"Max!" he shouted. He climbed back on board, tossing his beloved dog to safety just seconds before a keg of gunpowder caught fire and the ship exploded.

In the lifeboats, the other humans looked on in horror. They were sure the prince was lost forever!

But Ariel spotted Eric as he clung to a piece of wood. A second later, he lost his grip and sank below the surface.

Ariel dove down and caught him, swimming with all her might until she reached the surface. She didn't know much about humans, but she knew one thing for sure—they couldn't breathe underwater!

It was past dawn by the time Ariel managed to

drag Eric's limp body onto the sandy beach of a
deserted cove. The storm had passed, though clouds
still dotted the sky overhead.

"Is he—dead?" Ariel asked anxiously, staring
down at the human.

Scuttle flew down to help. "It's hard to say," the
seagull said thoughtfully, examining Eric's foot for
signs of life. "I can't make out a heartbeat."

Just then, the prince's lips parted and he sighed.
Ariel gasped. He was alive!

She stared at him. He was so handsome! She

longed to know more about
him—what would it be
like to know him, to be
part of his world? She
found herself singing
to him in her magical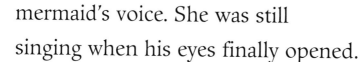
mermaid's voice. She was still
singing when his eyes finally opened.

Eric had no idea where he was. Who was the
beautiful girl staring down at him? The sun was in
his eyes, so he couldn't see her very well. But he
could hear her! Her voice was like an angel. . . .

Suddenly, there was a bark and the sound of
voices from the edge of the cove. Someone was
coming!

Ariel panicked. She couldn't let the other humans
find her here. What would they do if they saw her?
All her father's warnings flashed through her mind.

Leaving the prince on the beach, she dove below
the safety of the waves.

MONTH OF THE SHELL, FIFTH DAY OF THE RED ALGAE

W hat is happening to me? Diary, if you only knew. Since the first moment I saw Prince Eric, my whole life began to feel different. Part of me wishes I'd stayed with him, there on that beach, even though I wasn't sure what would happen next. But all I could do was watch from a distance as his friend Grimsby found him. Oh, and Max, too, of course.

Thinking about how he risked his own life to save Max makes me shiver. How can someone who would do that be a barbarian? Oh, how I wish Daddy could have

seen it! But I can never tell him. He would be so angry—I can't imagine what he'd do. I'm just happy that Sebastian agreed not to tell. I think he's hoping this is the end of the adventure.

But I can't help wishing it's just the beginning. I can't stop thinking about Eric—my sisters are starting to give me strange looks and muttering about my dreamy eyes and my humming. I can't help myself! What a strange feeling, when Prince Eric's eyes looked into mine. It was as if he knew me—knew me better than anyone else ever has.

But what can I do about it? Eric and I come from different worlds. I live under the water. He lives on land. I have fins, he has legs. What can possibly come of this? I feel so confused. . . . I wish I could talk to my sisters. They're older than me, and they know more about love. But they would only go running to Daddy if they heard I was falling in love with a human.

I know! I'll go talk to my mother's wise old nursemaid, Crystalla. She has always kept all of my deepest secrets and given me advice. I know I can trust her.

I think I'll go right this minute. Until later, Diary . . .

THE SECRET
OF THE SEA WITCH

Crystalla knew everything there was to know about life in the sea, and even quite a bit about life on land. She had lived many, many years in King Triton's palace, caring for the young members of the royal family. She had retired from her official duties before Ariel was born, but still shared her advice and wisdom freely with anyone who asked.

Ariel had always been her favorite of Triton's daughters. Her spirit and energy reminded Crystalla of the late queen. "Hello, sweetheart," she said fondly when Ariel swam in to greet her.

"Hi, Crystalla," Ariel said softly.

Crystalla peered at her. "Is something wrong, Ariel?" It seemed as if the little mermaid had something on her mind.

"Oh, no, Crystalla, everything's fine." Ariel let out a long, deep sigh.

Aha! Now Crystalla understood. She had seen these symptoms many times before. She smiled. "Ariel, my dear, you are in love!"

Ariel gasped. "How did you know?" she exclaimed. "I haven't told a soul! Oh, except Flounder—that little guppy didn't tell, did he?"

Crystalla laughed and stroked Ariel's cheek. "When you have white hair like mine and so many years behind you, you don't need to be told," she said. "I can see it in your eyes, dear child. But don't look so worried—sixteen years old is the perfect age for a mermaid to fall in love."

Ariel gulped. "Yes, but it's not that simple," she said nervously. "You see, um—that is, er . . ."

Suddenly, Ariel wasn't so sure she should tell. What if Crystalla disapproved? What if Crystalla *did* tell Ariel's father?

"What is it?" Crystalla asked. "Sweetheart, you know you can tell me anything, no matter what it is. Your secrets are mine."

Ariel sighed, knowing she had to trust someone. She would burst if she didn't share her news. Oh, Sebastian and Flounder knew, of course. But they couldn't possibly understand what she was feeling. Maybe Crystalla could.

"You're right," Ariel said, trying to keep her voice from trembling. "I *am* in love. With—with a human."

"What?" Crystalla cried, springing from her seat. "A human!" Her smile disappeared, and a strange expression took its place. "I certainly hope your father doesn't know about this!"

Ariel's heart froze. Oh, no! She had been wrong to trust Crystalla. "Please!" she cried desperately. "You can't tell Daddy about this. Please!"

Immediately, Crystalla's face softened. "Oh,

child," she murmured. "I'm sorry. I've frightened you. But don't be alarmed—I won't tell your father. As I promised, your secret is safe with me."

"Oh, thank you!" Ariel sank to the ocean floor in relief. "But why did you look so strange just now?"

Crystalla sighed. "Ah, Ariel," she said in a faraway voice. "It's just that—well, there are things you don't know about me. I was young once, too, and I liked to swim to the surface every once in a while to look around just like you do." She smiled. "Don't look so surprised. The whole kingdom has seen you staring up toward the surface. In any case, one day I spied a human man, the captain of a ship that often sailed over the kingdom."

She was silent for a moment, remembering the past.

"Yes?" Ariel said softly, curious to hear more. "And was your captain handsome?"

"Oh, yes." Crystalla smiled. "The handsomest

man I could imagine. I would have given anything to get close to him, to speak to him. . . . But the laws of the sea forbid it." She shook her head. "Your father was not the one who invented the rule against humans and merpeople mixing, Ariel. Such laws have been in place for many, many years." She sighed. "Unless your prince somehow trades his legs for fins, or you exchange your fins for legs, it's impossible."

Ariel frowned. Even Crystalla didn't seem to want to help her! "Well, fine!" she cried. "Then I'll just have to figure out a way to change my fins into legs!"

Crystalla chuckled. "But that is impossible, dear child," she said. "The only one who could do such a thing—the only one who *would* do such a thing—is Ursula, the sea witch."

"Ursula?" Ariel repeated slowly. "I—I have heard her name, of course. But nobody will tell me who she is or what she's done. They say I'm too young to understand."

"If you're old enough to fall in love, I suppose

you're old enough to hear Ursula's story," Crystalla said thoughtfully. "It begins many years ago, long before you were born, when your father was a young king with lots of enthusiasm but not much experience. Ursula lived in the palace then—she was a member of your dear mother's court. She was a strange girl, always getting herself into trouble. But nobody could have imagined all the trouble she would cause once she discovered the lure of dark magic."

Ariel's eyes widened. "Dark magic?"

"I'm afraid so." Crystalla shook her head sadly. "You see, Ursula wasn't satisfied with being just one of the many women of your mother's court; she wanted to be Queen of the Sea herself. She had hoped to marry Triton, but your mother captured his heart instead. So Ursula decided she would accuse King Triton of making a pact with the humans."

Ariel gasped. "Daddy?" she cried. "He would never do that! He thinks humans are barbarians."

"Yes," Crystalla agreed. "But Ursula can be very convincing, especially with the help of her magic. Many of the king's citizens started grumbling, saying that it was time for a new ruler."

"Oh, no!" Ariel was horrified. "Then what happened?"

"Fortunately, Sebastian overheard Ursula bragging to her pet eels, Flotsam and Jetsam," Crystalla said. "He told the king—and everybody else—and so

Ursula's plan was discovered before any real damage was done. She was banished from the kingdom forever, and from that day on, she has been known as the sea witch. She swore that sooner or later she would have her revenge on the king. Let's hope that day never comes."

Ariel agreed with that. She was so busy thinking about Crystalla's story that she forgot about her own problems for a little while.

And even when she remembered, she didn't feel quite as confused as she had before. It had helped to talk to someone about Eric—especially since Crystalla had once loved a human herself.

Of course, Crystalla had only admired her captain from afar. Ariel wasn't sure how, or when, but she was determined to do much more than that.

She had to find a way to see Eric again and tell him how she felt.

MONTH OF THE SHELL, FIFTH DAY OF THE RED ALGAE

*T*here is so much to write, and so little time!
Flotsam and Jetsam are waiting for me—I told
them I needed a moment to get ready.

But I should start at the beginning. I was still thinking
about my talk with Crystalla while Sebastian lectured me—
again—on why it was better to stay safely under the sea and
give up thinking about the surface world.

In the middle of it, Flounder pulled me away, saying
he had a big surprise. He led me to my secret hideaway—
and I almost exploded with joy. There was the statue of
Eric! It had fallen into the sea during the shipwreck,

and Flounder had found it and brought it there.

I was so excited I didn't hear Daddy coming until it was too late. I don't know how he found the hideaway, or how he knew about what had happened, but he did. He was furious—especially when I told him I was in love with Eric! Before I could stop him, he raised his trident and destroyed everything . . . even the statue.

My hand shakes as I write about it. I was too upset to think. All I could do as he left was cry.

A moment later, I heard a pair of strange voices:

"Poor child—she has a very serious problem. If only there was something we could do."

Then one of them said, "But there is something."

I looked up and saw two eels swimming around me. "Who are you?" I asked them nervously. There was something about their eyes—I wasn't sure I should trust them.

"Don't be scared," they told me. "We represent someone who can help you—someone who can make all your dreams come true. Just imagine: you and your prince, together forever."

How could they know? "I don't understand," I said.

"Ursula has great powers," they said with a hiss.

At first I was horrified. I remembered the terrible story Crystalla had told me earlier. I couldn't go to the sea witch for help! Not after what she'd done to Daddy.

Daddy . . . I looked around at the ruins of my beautiful collection. Daddy claimed he wanted me to be happy. But he seemed willing to destroy all my chances for true happiness.

Maybe Ursula was the answer, after all. Hadn't Crystalla said that the sea witch was the only one who might be able to change my fins into legs? Surely, it was worth a try. Right?

Well, the eels are still waiting. I don't want them to leave without me. So for now, farewell, Diary. May all my dreams come true before I write here next. . . .

SILENT LOVE

The closer Ariel got to Ursula's lair, the more nervous she felt. The water was getting darker and gloomier. Just outside the sea witch's cave, she saw a horrible sight. Hundreds of small, pitiful sea creatures anchored to the seafloor like limp water plants, with gaping jaws and huge, sad eyes that stared at Ariel as she passed. What were they? Ariel couldn't imagine. She wasn't sure she wanted to know.

Swimming past the imprisoned creatures as quickly as possible, she found herself looking in at a large, purple-skinned, white-haired, half-octopus figure.

"Come in, my child," Ursula greeted her, smiling. "We mustn't lurk in doorways. It's rude. One might question your upbringing." She chuckled. "Now then. You're here because you have a thing for this human, this prince fellow. Not that I blame you. He is quite a catch, isn't he? Well, angelfish," she

continued. "The solution to your problem is simple. The only way to get what you want is to give up your tail and become a human yourself."

Ariel gasped. Ursula had read her mind! "Can you do that?" she asked.

Ursula smiled. She could tell that the little mermaid had already made up her mind. It would be easy to reel her in—hook, line, and sinker. And that was just what the sea witch wanted. Sealing one of her sly magical deals with Triton's daughter would give her just the revenge she'd been looking for all these years!

"My dear, sweet child," Ursula said, assuringly, "that's what I do. It's what I live for, to help unfortunate merfolk like yourself—poor souls with no one else to turn to."

Then the sea witch laid out her terms. "Now, here's the deal," she said. "I will make you a potion that will turn you into a human for three days. Before the sun sets on the third day, you've got to get dear old Princie to fall in love with you. That is,

he's got to kiss you," the witch explained. "Not just any kiss—the kiss of true love. If he does kiss you before the sun sets on the third day, you'll remain human permanently."

Ursula waited until she saw Ariel's smile of joy. Oh, yes—hook, line, and sinker.

"But, if he doesn't," Ursula continued, "you turn back into a mermaid. And you belong to me. Have we got a deal?"

Ariel thought about what she had just heard. It sounded wonderful—she was sure Eric felt the same way she did. She had seen it in his eyes that day on the beach. They could be together forever!

Then she thought of something else. "If I become human, I'll never be with my father or sisters again."

"Life's full of tough choices," Ursula commented. "Oh, and there is one more thing—we haven't discussed the subject of payment. You can't get something for nothing, you know."

"But I don't have anything!" Ariel cried.

"I'm not asking much—just your voice," Ursula said.

"My voice?" Ariel put a hand to her throat, surprised. Without her voice, how could she explain things to Eric, tell him who she was? True, he had looked into her eyes—but he had just awakened from unconsciousness. There was no guarantee he would recognize her face. "But without my voice, how can I—?" she began.

The sea witch interrupted, already knowing what the little mermaid was thinking. "You'll have your looks and your pretty face," she assured her. Then she waved her hand and a scroll appeared, outlining the deal.

Ariel thought about

By signing this document, I hereby cede my voice to Ursula, the sea witch, for all eternity.
Sincerely,
in good faith,

_____

her father, her sisters, her home under the sea. Then she thought about Eric—about the possibility of never seeing him again.

That made up her mind. Taking the fish-bone pen Ursula offered, she signed her name at the bottom of the scroll. The ocean churned as Ursula captured Ariel's voice inside a magical shell and turned her tail to legs.

FIRST STEPS

Ariel was overwhelmed with so many feelings. First, of course, there were her new legs. They were so amazing, so wonderful! They weren't quite as easy to work as her familiar old tail, though. It took her a while to get the hang of standing upright on them without toppling over.

Then there were her friends. Oh, she had expected Scuttle to offer his help. And she knew that Flounder would be faithful, no matter what. But she hadn't been sure what Sebastian would do.

As soon as Ursula had mixed up her potion and

cast her spell, Ariel had suddenly discovered that she couldn't breathe underwater anymore. She'd choked and gasped, struggling to take a breath.

Luckily, Flounder and Sebastian were watching from the doorway. The two of them had rushed her up to the surface just in the nick of time. Then they had carried her to the same beach where she had taken the human prince. Scuttle had found them there and helped Ariel make a human-style dress out of an old abandoned sail. Flounder even dove down to retrieve Ariel's diary so she would have a way to record her adventures on land.

But Sebastian was worried and angry about what Ariel had done. At first he'd threatened to rush off and tell the sea king right away. He'd muttered something about finding Ursula and reversing the spell.

But then he'd seen Ariel's face. He

knew that if he went to the king now, she would be completely miserable for the rest of her life. Instead, he reluctantly offered to come along and help her if he could.

"What a soft shell I'm turning out to be," he muttered as she kissed him in thanks.

Another strange thing to get used to was not having a voice. She had to communicate with her friends with nods and smiles.

But she didn't care. It was worth it to be with Eric!

The sound of excited barking erupted from nearby. It was Max! He came running toward the cove.

Scuttle flew off, Flounder dived under the water, and Sebastian hopped inside a fold in Ariel's dress. Ariel was nervous as the dog bounded up to her.

Then Max greeted her with a big, slobbery lick— just as he had done back on the ship. He remembered her! Ariel was happy. Maybe Eric would remember her, too, and she wouldn't have to worry about not being able to explain. . . .

Just then, she heard a familiar voice shouting Max's name. It was Eric! He hurried down the beach, following Max's barks. He seemed startled to see Ariel sitting on a rock.

"Oh! Are you okay, miss?" he asked with concern. "I'm sorry if this knucklehead scared you. He's harmless really." He ruffled the dog's fur fondly, then peered at Ariel more closely. "You seem very familiar to me. Have we met?"

Ariel nodded eagerly. He remembered her!

"We have met! I knew it! You're the one I've been looking for!" he cried, grasping her hands as Max barked happily. "What's your name?"

Ariel opened her mouth to answer. Then she remembered—she couldn't speak. She put her hand to her throat, dismayed. She gestured, trying to make Eric understand.

It only took him a moment to catch on. "You can't speak?" His voice filled with disappointment. "Oh, then you couldn't be who I thought you were."

Ariel was disappointed, too. How could he not recognize her? She had thought that her eyes could reveal to the prince what her mouth could not express.

Nevertheless, she tried not to lose heart. There was still time.

MONTH OF THE SHELL, FIFTH DAY OF THE RED ALGAE

*O*h, how I've wished for this day! I have seen such wonderful things today—met so many wonderful people. Now that I'm unable to speak, I feel the need to write more than ever. I'm so grateful to Flounder for rescuing you, dear Diary!

Even though Eric doesn't know who I am, he has been so kind to me. He brought me back to his castle, where some maids helped me wash up and change into real human clothes. It feels so strange, all this cloth against my brand-new legs! Strange, but nice.

I was a little worried when I realized Sebastian had

disappeared along with the dress Scuttle made me. But he turned up at dinner, safe and sound.

Speaking of dinner, I had a few embarrassing moments at the table, thanks to Scuttle's mistakes. It turns out that dinglehoppers aren't for fixing one's hair—humans call them "forks" and use them to eat with. And when I saw Grimsby holding a snarfblatt, I blew into it, hoping to make music. Instead, black dust flew out, making a mess— it was really a pipe!

But Eric laughed in such a nice way that I didn't mind

my mistakes. He makes me feel so comfortable! Every moment I'm with him, I'm more certain than ever that I did the right thing. I only wish Daddy could understand. . . .

But no, I can't think about him right now. I need to fall asleep. Tomorrow, Eric promised to take me on a tour of the kingdom. That means the two of us will be alone together all day. That will be my chance to get Eric to kiss me! I'm a little nervous, but I know I can do it.

So now, time for bed. I'm sure all my dreams will be sweet ones!

KISS THE GIRL

Early the next morning, Ariel sat beside Eric in his carriage, ready for the marvelous sights that awaited her.

Everything was so new to her! To start with, Eric's carriage was pulled by a horse—a huge, wonderful creature that was nothing like a sea horse at all. The town square was filled with so many interesting things that she hardly knew where to look first.

And the music! Now that she had legs, it seemed

she could hardly stop dancing. As a band of musicians played, she dragged Eric out for a dance.

After that, they drove out of the village into the
countryside. Eric even let Ariel drive the carriage for
a while.

Finally, as the sun began to set, the two of them
set out in a rowboat on a peaceful lagoon. The
evening songs of crickets and frogs accompanied
them as they floated along. As he rowed, Eric was
overcome with an almost irresistible urge to kiss the
red-haired girl sitting across from him.

But that was silly. He hardly knew her! Besides, his heart belonged to another—the mysterious girl with the beautiful voice who had rescued him from the shipwreck.

To take his mind off his thoughts, he spoke to the girl. "You know, I feel really bad about not knowing your name," he told her. "Maybe I can guess." He thought for a second, guessing the first name that came to him. "Is it, uh—Mildred?"

He could tell that he was wrong right away by the look on her face. He laughed. It was amazing how much this girl could communicate without ever saying a word!

"How about Diana? Rachel?" he continued to guess.

Suddenly, as if spoken by a little voice out of nowhere, a name popped into his head—*"Ariel."*

"Ariel?" he said uncertainly. He had never heard that name before.

At the name, the girl's eyes lit up. She smiled and nodded happily, grabbing his hands.

"Ariel," he repeated, a little amazed that he'd managed to guess. Of course, he didn't have any idea that a little crab named Sebastian had just whispered the name into his ear! "That's kind of pretty," Eric went on.

He and Ariel smiled at each other as the boat floated on. Now that he knew her name, Eric felt closer to this girl than ever. Once again, he was gripped by the urge to let her know how he was feeling. He leaned toward Ariel, about to kiss her when . . .

SPLASH! Without warning, the boat overturned, dumping them both into the shallow water. That was the end of the romantic moment.

Ariel could hardly hide her disappointment. Why did this have to happen now, just when all her dreams were about to come true?

She didn't see Flotsam and Jetsam, Ursula's two eels, grinning with satisfaction and swimming away. They had capsized the rowboat. They knew that the sea witch didn't want Ariel to succeed. If she did, all of Ursula's plans for revenge would be ruined!

Back at the castle, Ariel stood on the balcony outside her room. She looked at the moon shining down on the sea and thought about the day she had just shared with Eric. Even though it made her feel sad to be away from her family and friends, she

couldn't help feel-
ing happy. She and
Eric were becom-
ing closer and
closer. He hadn't
kissed her yet, but
she still had
another whole day.

And she
planned to make
the most of it.

A Surprising Announcement

The next morning, Ariel was awakened by Scuttle's excited voice. He flapped in through the open window, calling her name.

"Ariel, wake up! I just heard the news!" he cried. "Congratulations, kiddo—we did it!"

As the little mermaid opened her eyes and looked at the seagull sleepily, Sebastian yawned and rubbed his eyes. "What is this idiot babbling about?" he grumbled.

"The whole town's buzzing about the prince getting himself hitched this afternoon!"

For a moment, Ariel wasn't sure what to think. Married? Eric was getting married? But then she realized what Scuttle meant. Eric wanted to marry *her!*

She smiled and spun around the room gleefully. After that almost-kiss yesterday, Ariel had thought she would have to work harder to convince Eric that she was the one for him. But he had figured it out on his own!

Not even taking the time to get dressed, she raced out of the room and down the stairs. She had never been so happy in all her life.

MONTH OF THE SHELL, SIXTH DAY OF THE RED ALGAE

I *hadn't even made it down the steps when I saw him . . . when I saw* them. *Eric—my Eric—was arm in arm with a beautiful girl with long, dark hair. At first, I didn't understand. Then I heard Grimsby saying something about how he was mistaken, that Eric's mystery maiden from the beach really did exist.*

But how could this be? I was the girl from the beach! Surely, Eric had to realize that by now. . . .

But no. I heard him say that he and this other girl, Vanessa, were to be married—today! Their wedding ship would depart at sunset.

I could feel my heart breaking. Just when all my dreams seemed about to come true, all hope was lost!

I came here to the beach to write down my thoughts and figure out what to do. But what can I do except stare out at the sea I left behind? I've never felt so lonely or hopeless in all my—

Ariel stopped writing in midsentence. Was she seeing things, or was that a merperson emerging from the waves? She gasped.

It was Crystalla! She couldn't believe the old nursemaid would defy King Triton's orders.

But sure enough, it was her old friend. "Oh, my child!" Crystalla exclaimed as Ariel raced into the shallow water to hug her. "Flounder just told me everything. You must come with me—perhaps together we can change the sea witch's mind."

Ariel looked puzzled. For a moment, she wasn't sure what Crystalla meant.

"Hurry—before the sun sets and your time runs out," Crystalla urged. "We still have a few hours. I know things about Ursula that you can't even imagine. If there's a way to convince her to return you to your old form, we'll find it."

Now Ariel understood. Was it possible? Could Crystalla convince Ursula to turn Ariel back into a mermaid?

But wouldn't that be like admitting she'd been wrong to try? Ariel glanced at the castle behind her. It hadn't been wrong. Maybe the wrong thing would be to give up now, to go back on her vow to see this through.

Ariel shook her head no. She needed to do this on her own. She hugged Crystally tightly.

Leaving Crystalla behind, Ariel headed back toward the castle.

VANESSA

As the afternoon wore on, the wedding ship was prepared for its evening cruise. While the castle's staff bustled around the bride, Ariel watched from a distance.

How had it happened? How had the mysterious Vanessa managed to steal her true love's heart in just one day?

She wished she could talk to Prince Eric, to try to explain. Her voice! Why had she given up her voice?

She glanced at the diary in her lap. For once, she

hadn't wanted to write about her feelings. She hadn't written one word since that morning.

But maybe writing was the answer. Maybe she could write down her true identity, her story, and show it to Eric!

But no. Her shoulders slumped as she realized that wouldn't work. Even if she could find Eric and convince him to read such a thing on his wedding day, he would only laugh. A mute girl who combs her hair with a fork and says she's a mermaid—it was too crazy.

Besides, he was in love with someone else.

Soon the ship was ready. Ariel was invited to the wedding, but she hid behind a pillar as the wedding party boarded the boat and the sailors pulled up the anchor. She couldn't bear to watch Eric marry someone else. She would just wait here until sunset, when the sea witch arrived to claim her prize.

As the wedding ship sailed out of the port, Ariel sat crying on the dock. Sebastian and Flounder were

with her, but neither could think of a single thing to say to make their friend feel better.

Suddenly, a terrible squawk interrupted the sad scene. It was Scuttle. He had just peeked in a window of the wedding ship and seen Vanessa getting ready for the ceremony. But when she'd looked in the mirror, Scuttle had seen her true face reflected in the glass—it was the sea witch! She had disguised herself as a beautiful human girl and used Ariel's captive voice, which she held in a locket around her neck, to win Prince Eric's heart! And it had worked—the prince had thought Vanessa was the girl from the beach who had saved him.

"What are we going to do?" Flounder exclaimed.

Ariel didn't waste a moment. It was almost sunset. In a few minutes, it would be too late. Ursula would have her soul—and Eric, too. She couldn't let that happen!

She raced across the dock and dove into the sea, forgetting for a moment that she couldn't swim as easily now with legs as with her tail. Sebastian came to

her rescue, rolling a large barrel into the water. Ariel grabbed it, and Flounder pulled the barrel toward the ship.

"I've got to get to the sea king," Sebastian muttered anxiously. "He must know about this!"

"What about me?" Scuttle asked, wondering what he could do to help.

"Find a way to stall that wedding!" Sebastian cried as he leaped into the water.

Scuttle took his orders seriously. He roused every bird, fish, lobster, and seal he could find and led them to the ship. The ceremony had already begun, and Scuttle wasted no time. He and a gang of birds dive-bombed the bride and groom. Sea creatures leaped on board from every direction, splashing the guests. Soon the entire ship was in chaos!

Meanwhile, Flounder was struggling to pull the barrel that Ariel was leaning on. Ariel knew he was trying his best, but her heart pounded nervously as she looked at the setting sun. It was halfway below the horizon. She would never make it in time!

But she was wrong. They finally reached the ship, and Ariel climbed on board. She was greeted by a scene of total mayhem. Scuttle and some of the other creatures were chasing Vanessa.

Vanessa screamed as Scuttle pulled at the shell necklace containing Ariel's voice. The string snapped and the shell tumbled to the deck, where it broke into dozens of pieces. There was a flash of

light, and the sound of sweet singing. Freed from its magical prison, Ariel's voice floated up until it found its true home in Ariel's own throat.

The little mermaid began to sing.

"Ariel?" Eric said uncertainly when he heard that haunting, familiar song coming from the red-haired girl.

"Eric!" Ariel cried happily. Now, at last, she would be able to explain! It seemed too good to be true!

It was at that moment, just as Eric bent to kiss Ariel at last, that the sun dipped below the horizon. It was too late!

Still disguised as Vanessa, Ursula laughed in victory as Ariel slipped from Eric's arms. Ariel fell to the deck as her legs transformed back into a tail. Then, Ursula changed back into her true form and grabbed Ariel. The wedding guests gasped in horror and fear.

"So long, lover boy!" the sea witch called out to Eric as she threw herself into the sea, dragging Ariel with her.

A TERRIBLE TRADE

As they sped toward the bottom of the sea, King Triton appeared before them. "Ursula! Stop!" he shouted. "Let her go!"

"Not a chance, Triton. She's mine now," Ursula retorted. "We made a deal."

The sea witch unfurled the scroll that Ariel had signed. Such a contract couldn't be broken by anyone, not even the sea king.

"But I might be willing to make an exchange," Ursula said. She offered Ariel's soul in exchange for Triton's own—along with the trident that would

make Ursula the queen of the sea at last.

Ariel looked on in horror as her father raised his
trident. He wouldn't—he couldn't! But a second later,
it was done. He signed his own name on the scroll
over Ariel's. Ursula cackled in triumph as the powerful King Triton shrank down, down, down until he
had become one of those pitiful little sea creatures
like those outside Ursula's cave.

"Your Majesty!" Sebastian said sadly.

"Daddy!" Ariel cried. She couldn't believe her

father had made such a sacrifice for her. For the second time that day, she felt as if her heart was breaking.

"At last it's mine!" Ursula exclaimed as she picked up Triton's crown and trident.

Suddenly, something sliced through the water. It was a harpoon! Ursula cried out in fury as she turned and saw Prince Eric swimming behind her. He had followed her deep into the ocean, determined to save his beloved Ariel.

"Eric, look out!" Ariel cried.

"After him!" Ursula shouted at Flotsam and Jetsam.

"Say good-bye to your sweetheart," Ursula told Ariel as she aimed the trident at Eric.

But Ariel wasn't ready to say good-bye just yet. Instead, she grabbed Ursula's hair. The trident's bolt shot off-course. Instead of hitting Eric, it struck the two eels, destroying them!

Now Ursula was *really* furious. Gripping the trident, she called on all her magic powers. She grew larger and larger until she was twice the size of Eric's ship. Ariel and Eric, clinging to each other, looked on in horror.

The sea churned around them as Ursula whipped up the surface of the water with her enormous tentacles, raising waves as high as mountains. Suddenly, a gigantic whirlpool arose from the bottom of the sea. As Ariel got sucked into it, the sea witch aimed the trident at the little mermaid, shooting bolt after bolt at her. Ariel dodged the first few, but she knew it was only a matter of time until the sea witch destroyed her.

But Eric hadn't given up. The whirlpool had brought the wreck of his old ship to the surface. Climbing aboard, he spun the rudder until the sharp remnant of the ship's broken mast was aiming straight at the sea witch. By the time Ursula turned to see what was coming, it was too late.

The terrifying scream of the sea witch echoed throughout the undersea kingdom. She fell with a mighty splash. A moment later, the sea closed over her forever.

HAPPILY EVER AFTER

It was all over. The end of the sea witch meant an end to all of her dark magic. As the trident sank to the ocean floor, King Triton regained his true form. So did all the other souls of the poor sea creatures Ursula had imprisoned over the years.

But even though she'd helped defeat the terrible sea witch, Ariel couldn't feel completely happy. Perched on a rock, she watched Eric, who

was lying exhausted on the shore.

Ursula had been defeated. But nothing else had changed. Ariel was still a mermaid, and Eric was still a man. Would they now have to live the rest of their lives apart, despite all that had happened?

Suddenly, there was a magical golden flash. Her fins tingled, and to her amazement, she saw them turning back into legs!

She turned and saw her father smiling at her, holding his trident. Of course! His good magic was

much more powerful than Ursula's dark magic had
ever been. And finally, he had
used it to give her the
one thing she had
always wanted.

Maybe he did
understand,
after all!

MONTH OF THE SEA HORSE, SECOND DAY OF THE SEA STAR

*T*he next time I write, I'll use the human calendar, but for now I want to enjoy the things that remind me of my old home under the sea. Now that I no longer feel myself a prisoner there, I find I can remember that world with love.

I can hardly believe Eric and I are married! We just held the ceremony here on this ship so that Daddy and the rest of my undersea family and friends could be part of it. I've never been so happy!

Still, it's sad to say good-bye to everyone. Of course,

I'll still be able to see them sometimes on the beach. But it won't be the same.

A little while ago, Crystalla came to say good-bye. We found a quiet spot off the side of the ship. Our relationship has always been special, so I wanted our good-bye to be special, too.

That's when she gave me her wedding gift—a pair of earrings made of the whitest, most precious pearls from under the sea. She told me they'd once belonged to my mother. It was the most wonderful gift I could imagine—I couldn't help crying a little. But they weren't really tears of sadness. They were tears of joy for having such wonderful friends in my life—both on land and under the sea.

I'll never forget the world that I come from. But I'm ready to start my life in a new world—Eric's world, the wonderful, amazing world of humans, which is about to become my world, too.

I guess sometimes dreams really do come true!

THE STORY OF
Jasmine

A Golden Cage

Once upon a time, in a faraway land, there was a city called Agrabah. It was a place of mystery and enchantment. Narrow streets and twisted alleyways ran past houses of all shapes and sizes. Most of them led to the marketplace, where it was possible to find almost anything for sale—fresh figs, woven baskets, colorful silks, and much more. People from all over the kingdom gathered there, and the sounds of bargaining, shouting, and laughter filled the air.

The Sultan's palace overlooked it all. Although it

had a fine view of Agrabah, the palace was separated from the city's smells, sounds, and people by high walls. Nobody could go in or out without passing the Sultan's guards.

Inside that palace lived Princess Jasmine, the daughter of the Sultan. Jasmine was beautiful and spirited, with long, raven-colored hair and curious brown eyes. She had everything her father's riches could buy—mouthwatering foods, beautiful clothes, many loyal servants. Yet she was not happy. . . .

One sunny afternoon, three days before her sixteenth birthday, Princess Jasmine sat beside a fountain in the palace garden. Her pet tiger, Rajah, had just chased away another prince who had come to seek her hand in marriage. Her father, the Sultan, was very upset.

The Sultan loved his daughter. He wanted her
to choose a suitor because it was the law—Princess
Jasmine had to be married to a prince by her
sixteenth birthday. But he also wanted her to find
a husband so she would have someone to take care
of her.

But Jasmine didn't see what the big hurry was.
"If I *do* marry, I want it to be for love," she told her
father. "Please try to understand—I've never done a
thing on my own. I've never had any real friends!"

At that, Rajah looked up in surprise, and Jasmine laughed.

"Except you, Rajah," she assured the tiger with a pat. Then she turned to her father again, hoping he would understand this time. "I've never even been outside the palace walls!"

The Sultan was shocked. "But, Jasmine, you're a princess!" he exclaimed. Princesses didn't just wander around outside. Agrabah could be dangerous. Why couldn't Jasmine see that?

Jasmine frowned. "Then maybe I don't want to be a princess anymore!" she cried.

"Oooh!" The Sultan clenched his fists. Why did she have to be so stubborn about this? "Allah forbid *you* should have any daughters!" he cried, throwing his hands in the air.

Jasmine sighed and skimmed her fingers across the surface of the water in the fountain as her father stormed away. He just didn't understand. All he thought about was that stupid law.

"The law is wrong!" Jasmine murmured as she

stared at her reflection in the fountain.

She sighed again. If only her mother were still
alive, maybe she would
understand. But she had
died when Jasmine
was a baby. Jasmine
only knew her
mother's face from
the framed picture
she carried with her
everywhere she went.

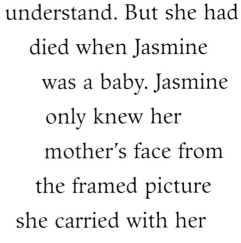

Everyone said that Jasmine looked just like her
mother. Jasmine only wished she'd had a chance to
know her. Instead, she had been raised by kind and
caring nursemaids and other servants. She loved
them all—especially her most faithful and dear old
nursemaid, Amina—but it just wasn't the same.

Jasmine had tried many times to explain her feelings to her father, but it was hopeless. He didn't
seem to understand his daughter at all. Nobody did.
Sometimes Jasmine felt just as trapped as the doves

who lived in the elegant aviary just beyond the fountain. Like the doves, she lived in a golden cage—she could see the outside world, but she wasn't allowed to experience it.

A sudden impulse overtook her, and she jumped to her feet and approached the aviary. She stared at the birds. They were well fed and cared for by the palace staff. But was that enough for them? Did they long to soar into the blue sky overhead—the sky they could see through the bars of their beautiful golden prison?

She opened the door on the side of the cage. The doves hesitated for a moment, cooing uncertainly. Then, in a burst of white, they exploded out of the aviary and soared into the fresh open air.

Jasmine followed the white cloud of birds with her gaze until they were lost in the distance.

Finally, the princess was smiling.

Meanwhile, in the throne room, the Sultan was still trying to figure out why his daughter was so upset. Why didn't she want to get married? It was the way things were done!

"I don't know where she gets it from. Her mother wasn't nearly so picky. . . ." he grumbled to himself.

At that moment, the Sultan's grand vizier entered the room. The Sultan smiled when he saw him.

"Ah, Jafar!" he cried. "My most trusted adviser. I am in desperate need of your wisdom."

Jafar bowed to the Sultan with a smug smile. "My life is but to serve you, my lord," he said.

"It's this suitor business," the Sultan explained with a sigh. He had discussed the problem with Jafar many times before. "Jasmine refuses to choose a husband. I'm at my wit's end!"

Jafar was prepared for this moment. "Now then . . . perhaps I can divine a solution to this thorny problem," he said. "But it would require the use of the Mystic Blue Diamond." He fixed his gaze on the enormous aqua-colored stone on the Sultan's finger.

The Sultan gasped in surprise. "My ring?" he said, glancing down at the stone. "But . . . it's been in the family for years."

Once again, Jafar was prepared. He lifted his cobra-headed staff. Its red eyes began to glow.

"Don't worry," Jafar said soothingly. "Everything will be fine."

The Sultan stared into the cobra's eyes. His eyes began to glaze over. Soon he was completely hypnotized by Jafar's magic.

Jafar smiled in triumph as the Sultan handed over his ring. Now that he had the Mystic Blue Diamond, Jafar would finally be able to locate the treasure he'd been seeking for years—a treasure hidden deep within the legendary Cave of Wonders.

Many had sought the gold, jewels, and other riches that lay within the cave. But Jafar was not interested in those things. The only thing that interested him was a common lamp, similar to those that could be found in homes all over the kingdom. But the lamp was much more than what it seemed. It was not the humble outside that mattered, but what was within.

The trouble was that the Cave of Wonders was guarded by a fierce tiger-spirit. Jafar had tried to enter the cave once before with the help of a petty thief named Gazeem. But the tiger-spirit's voice had boomed, "Only one may enter here—one whose worth lies far within: a diamond in the rough."

When Gazeem stepped forward into the cave, the tiger's mouth instantly closed up and the cave disappeared into the sand. Apparently, Gazeem was not the diamond in the rough. But with the help of the Mystic Blue Diamond, Jafar was determined to find the one who could enter the cave and use him to get what he wanted.

Once inside Jafar's secret laboratory, he and his parrot, Iago, brought out a magical hourglass, which held the all-seeing "sands of time." By activating the Mystic Blue Diamond's powers, the sands parted in the hourglass, revealing to Jafar the diamond in the rough—a boy in the Agrabah marketplace.

Outside in the garden, Jasmine was still thinking about her own problems. As she stared at her reflection in the fountain, she pictured her father in the water. She knew he wanted what was best for her. But he didn't seem to understand what she truly wanted.

What was she going to do? She couldn't stay
here and marry one of the pompous, boring princes
who came to call. And yet she didn't seem to have
any other choice. Or did she . . . ?

AN ADVENTURE FIT
FOR A PRINCESS

I have to get out of here! Jasmine thought as she walked through the palace gardens. She looked around at the familiar sights. She knew every path, every tree, every blossom in the flower beds. The palace and these gardens had made up her entire world. Until now . . .

"Princess! Princess Jasmine!"

It was the servants calling her name—probably so they could help her dress for dinner. But instead of walking toward the voices, Jasmine hurried in the opposite direction.

Soon the princess reached the palace kitchens, which lay near the gate where the servants and other workers entered and exited the palace. She paused and glanced longingly at the heavy wooden doors built into the smooth walls. If only she could simply open those doors and walk outside. . . .

But she knew that was impossible. The doors were guarded at every moment, day and night. She would never be able to escape that way.

However, she had a different plan in mind. Every day, women from the marketplace arrived, carrying large baskets of food—luscious fruits, crisp vegetables, sweet dates, fresh fish—that they wanted to sell to the palace cooks. Jasmine hid behind a shrub and waited, knowing that another market woman would be arriving soon.

Sure enough, a woman soon arrived at the gates. She was dressed in a plain brown cloak and carrying a basket of figs. Jasmine waited until the woman passed close by her hiding place. Then she reached out and pulled her behind the shrub.

The woman cried out in terror. "Allah save me!" she exclaimed fearfully.

"Don't be frightened!" Jasmine whispered, shushing her. "I won't hurt you. I only ask a favor."

The woman stared at her. "Who are you, beautiful lady?" she asked. "What do you want of me?"

For once, Jasmine was glad that almost no one in the kingdom had ever seen her except at a great distance. She didn't want the woman to know that she was really the princess.

"My name doesn't matter," she said. "Only my request. Please, I beg of you—may I have your cloak?"

The woman seemed surprised at the request. "My—my cloak?" she said, pulling it a bit tighter around her. "But why? Your garments are much finer."

"Yes, but I really need your cloak," Jasmine said. "It's very important."

Still the woman hesitated. "I would surely help you if I could, fine lady. But I have no other cloak besides this one."

Jasmine knew that if she revealed her identity as the princess, the woman would hand over the cloak without question. But she didn't want to do that. The whole point of this adventure was to escape her life as a princess.

Instead, she slipped the ring she was wearing off

her finger. "Please," she said, holding it out to the woman, "take this in exchange. You can sell it and buy yourself a new cloak."

The woman gaped at the beautiful stone set in the ring. She had never seen such a fine jewel. Surely, it would buy her a thousand new cloaks, made of silk and fine linen.

Reaching out with trembling fingers, the woman touched the ring. "But I couldn't," she whispered. "It's worth so much more than my simple cloak."

"I know." Jasmine smiled at the woman's honesty. She pressed the ring into her hand. "But, please, I beg of you, accept the trade."

When the woman looked into Jasmine's eyes, she saw desperation there—perhaps her humble cloak really was worth more than jewels to the pretty young lady. Setting down her basket of figs, the woman quickly slipped off the cloak.

Many hours later, just as dawn's first rays touched the horizon, a figure wrapped in a plain brown cloak slipped through the palace gardens.

The figure paused beside a tall tree growing next to the high garden wall. When the figure looked up, the cloak's hood fell back. It was Jasmine.

She reached up her hands to climb the tree. Just then, she felt a tug on the hem of the cloak. It was Rajah.

Jasmine smiled sadly at her friend. "I'm sorry, Rajah," she said, "but I can't stay here and have my life lived for me. I'll miss you!"

She hugged the tiger. Then Rajah stood beside the wall to help her up the first few feet to the tree. He watched sadly as she climbed to the top of the wall.

Pausing, she glanced back for one more look at the gardens—and one more smile for her old friend. She blew Rajah a kiss. "Good-bye!"

Moments later, Jasmine found herself wandering through unfamiliar streets. At first, things were quiet. But as morning arrived, Agrabah came to life.

Jasmine wasn't sure where to look first. There were interesting sights to see everywhere she

turned! Then she reached the marketplace, and found even more new sights, sounds, and smells.

She saw sword swallowers, fire breathers, snake charmers, and even a fakir who could lie for hours on a bed of nails. As she walked around, the street vendors tried to sell her everything under the sun.

"A pretty necklace for a pretty lady!" one man crooned as she passed his stall. Jasmine smiled politely and kept on walking.

Even more fascinating than the goods in the market stalls were the people who were milling about—so many people! Jasmine had known only the servants and the residents of the palace. She didn't know anything about the rest of her father's subjects. As she passed a fruit stand, she saw a little boy. His big eyes were fixed on a basket of juicy apples.

Jasmine stopped and smiled at the little boy. "Oh,

you must be hungry," she said, picking up the plumpest, juiciest-looking apple and handing it to him. "Here you go."

All of a sudden, a gruff voice from behind her yelled, "You'd better be able to pay for that!"

Startled, Jasmine turned and saw a large, rough-looking man scowling at her. "Pay?" she whispered, suddenly remembering that she wasn't in the palace anymore. Out here, nobody knew that she was the princess.

"No one steals from my cart!" the fruit seller exclaimed angrily.

"I'm sorry, sir," Jasmine said, feeling frightened for the first time since scaling the palace wall. "I don't have any money."

"Thief!" the man shouted.

Jasmine backed away, realizing she'd made a big mistake. "Please, if you let me go to the palace, I can get some from the Sultan. . . ."

The man grabbed her by the wrist. "Do you know what the penalty is for stealing?" he cried, lifting his sword.

Jasmine froze in terror. How had she gotten herself into this mess?

She almost closed her eyes as the man's sword started down toward her. But at the last moment, a hand shot out and stopped it.

"Thank you, kind sir!" a new voice cried out happily. "I'm so glad you found her!" A dark-haired boy with sparkling eyes was standing there. He looked at Jasmine. "I've been looking for you."

Jasmine blinked. What was going on? She had never seen this boy before in her life—yet he acted as if he knew her. "What are you doing?" she whispered to him uncertainly.

He winked. "Just play along," he whispered back.

Meanwhile, the fruit seller had lowered his sword, looking confused. "You know this girl?" he asked the boy.

The boy shrugged. "Sadly, yes. She is my sister." He leaned closer and twirled one finger beside his head. "She's a little crazy."

Jasmine frowned for a moment, insulted. But then she realized that this must be part of the boy's plan.

"She said she knew the Sultan," the fruit seller said suspiciously.

"She thinks the monkey is the Sultan," the boy replied, pointing to the pet monkey sitting on his shoulder.

Jasmine decided she'd better play along, as the boy had said. "Oh, wise Sultan!" she cried, bowing before the little monkey. "How may I serve you?"

Out of the corner of her eye, she saw the boy secretly swipe an apple from another pile. He handed it to the fruit seller, pretending it was the apple Jasmine had given to the little boy. Then he grabbed Jasmine by the arm.

"Come along, sis," he said. "Time to see the doctor."

Jasmine was starting to have fun with this game.

"Oh, hello, doctor. How are you?" she said, smiling at a nearby camel before the boy dragged her away to make their escape.

A few minutes later, the boy, the monkey, and Jasmine were climbing stairs in an abandoned building. The boy, whose name was Aladdin, was used to making narrow escapes through the alleyways of Agrabah. He was curious about the girl he'd rescued. She wasn't from around here—he lived on the streets and knew almost everybody. Who was she? Where had she come from?

But first they had to reach the safety of his hideout. He helped the girl climb over fallen stones and loose boards. But when it was time to leap over an alleyway between two rooftops, she refused his help. Grabbing a pole, she vaulted over the alley herself.

Aladdin smiled, impressed with the stranger's

spirit. He could
already tell
she wasn't
like any girl
he'd ever met
before.

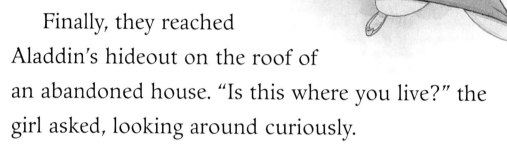

Finally, they reached
Aladdin's hideout on the roof of
an abandoned house. "Is this where you live?" the
girl asked, looking around curiously.

"Yep! Just me and Abu," Aladdin replied, gesturing to the monkey. "We come and go as we please."

"That sounds fabulous," the girl said with a sigh.

Aladdin was surprised—he
liked his home, but it was far
from fancy. "So where are you
from?" he asked.

"What does it matter?"
Jasmine replied, staring toward the palace in the
distance. "I ran away, and I am *not* going back."

"Why not?" Aladdin asked.

"My father is forcing me to get married," Jasmine explained.

Aladdin gulped. Married? For some reason, the idea of this girl getting married disturbed him.

Meanwhile, Jasmine was wondering what had come over her. How could she sit here, telling all her most private secrets to a stranger? Still, there was something about the boy that made her want to trust him. . . .

"May Allah grant you his protection on this day, Princess Jas—"

Amina's words broke off with a gasp. The princess's loyal servant had just drawn back the curtains on Jasmine's royal bed to reveal that it was empty!

"What is it?" A young handmaiden heard the older woman's gasp and came to see what was wrong. "Oh, no!"

Soon every maid in the palace was searching for the missing princess. But she was nowhere to be found. With a heavy heart, Amina went in search of the Sultan to give him the terrible news.

Instead, she found Jafar just outside the throne room. "What is it, woman?" the vizier snarled impatiently.

Amina trembled as she bowed. All the servants were afraid of Jafar's foul temper and sneaky ways. "It's the princess, sir," she whispered. "This morning, I entered her chamber as usual, but. . . ."

She went on to explain. As she spoke, Jafar stroked his beard thoughtfully. The princess missing? Interesting. Perhaps he could use this to distract the Sultan from other matters—such as wondering what Jafar was really doing with the Mystic Blue Diamond. He would have to save this news for a time when it best served him. . . . He realized the servant woman was still speaking.

". . . And so, I was about to inform the Sultan of the terrible news," she whispered timidly, bowing again.

"Never mind," Jafar told her firmly. "I shall inform his lordship myself. Do not worry yourself about it anymore. The princess shall be found."

Amina was surprised at the vizier's mild response. She had been expecting him to throw her in the palace dungeon for delivering such terrible news. "Yes, sir," she said with a final bow. "Thank you, sir." With that, she scurried away.

Jafar entered the throne room, where the Sultan was sitting on his throne, worrying over Jasmine's marriage.

"Oh, hello, Jafar." The Sultan greeted his adviser, distracted by his worries. "Everything all right in the palace this morning?"

"But of course, sire," Jafar said to him smoothly. "Everything is fine. Just fine."

Captured!

As Jasmine and Aladdin gazed at the view of the faraway palace, there was a shout from the stairway leading to the rooftop. It was the palace guards!

Jasmine and Aladdin both jumped to their feet. "They're after me!" the two of them cried at once.

Then they stared at each other in surprise. "They're after *you*?" they said at the same time.

But there was no time to discuss it. So they ran. But the palace guards were everywhere! Soon there was no place left to run.

Aladdin looked over the edge of the roof. Maybe there was a way. . . .

"Do you trust me?" he asked.

Jasmine stared at him. "What?"

"Do you trust me?" Aladdin repeated.

Jasmine looked into his eyes. She could see something in them—something honest and true. "Yes," she said.

He took her hand, and they jumped. Seconds later, Aladdin, Jasmine, and Abu landed safely in a soft pile of milled grain. The three of them leaped up and started racing through the marketplace.

But Rasoul, the head palace guard, and his men didn't give up. Jafar had ordered them to find Aladdin—the Mystic Blue Diamond had revealed him to be the only person who could enter the Cave of Wonders.

"We just keep running into each other, don't we, street rat?" Rasoul sneered as he grabbed Aladdin. "It's the dungeon for you, boy!"

Aladdin shouted for Jasmine to run. But she stepped forward, furious at the way the guards were manhandling her new friend. Her father would never approve of such behavior!

"Let him go!" she demanded.

Rasoul laughed, not recognizing her. "Looky here, men!" he cried. "A street mouse!"

"Unhand him! By order of the princess!" Jasmine let the hood of her cloak fall to her shoulders, revealing her face.

"Princess Jasmine!" Rasoul exclaimed, shocked. Immediately, he and the other guards bowed in respect.

"The princess?" Aladdin said as his jaw dropped open in amazement.

"What are you doing outside the palace? And with this street rat . . .?" Rasoul continued.

"That's not your concern. Do as I command. Release him!" Jasmine ordered.

"I would, Princess," Rasoul said apologetically. "Except my orders come from Jafar. You'll have to take it up with him."

Jasmine's eyes narrowed. She should have known Jafar was behind this outrage! "Believe me, I will!" she cried.

Now that she had been seen, Jasmine knew her adventure was over. She didn't have time to worry about that, though. She was too concerned about what might become of her new friend at the hands of the palace guards. She had heard stories from the servants of the terrible things that sometimes went on in the palace dungeons.

Rasoul and several of his guards dragged Aladdin away. Others stayed behind to accompany the princess. As she passed a group of children playing in the street, she felt a tug on her cloak. She turned and saw the little boy she had given the apple to a little while before.

"Thank you, miss," he responded shyly.

"Why, hello again," she said with a smile. "What's your name?"

"Kerim," the boy answered. "Why are those guards following you? Did you steal another apple?"

"No." Jasmine laughed. "They're accompanying me to the palace."

"The palace!" The boy's eyes widened. "Do you live there? Have you ever seen the princess? They say she is very beautiful."

"Yes, I've seen her many times," Jasmine answered truthfully, hiding a smile. "Maybe you'll see her yourself one day."

"Oh!" The boy looked amazed at the idea.

Jasmine then realized that Rasoul and his prisoner were out of sight. She had to speak with Jafar before anything terrible happened to her friend. "I have to go now, Kerim. But one day I'll take you to the palace to meet the princess. I promise."

With a wave to the little boy, she hurried on her way, with the other guards in tow.

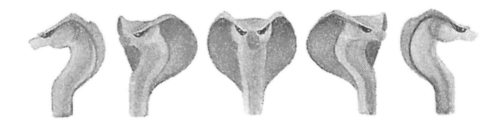

Back at the palace, Jasmine quickly located the grand vizier. She glared at him as he bowed to her. Although Jafar was her father's closest adviser, Jasmine didn't trust him one bit.

"Princess," he greeted her. "How may I be of service to you?"

"The guards just took a boy from the market—on your orders," she snapped.

Jafar shrugged, seemingly surprised at her anger. "Your father has charged me with keeping peace in Agrabah," he said. "The boy was a criminal."

"What was his crime?" Jasmine demanded.

Once again, Jafar feigned surprise. "Why, kidnapping the princess, of course," he purred. He was pleased with the way things had worked out. Jasmine's escape had given him the perfect excuse to snatch Aladdin without anyone's complaining—not even that ridiculous softy of a sultan.

Jasmine gasped in horror. "He didn't kidnap me!" she cried. "I ran away!"

"Oh, dear, how frightfully upsetting," Jafar lied.

"Had I but known . . . the boy's sentence has already been carried out."

"What sentence?" Jasmine asked fearfully.

"Death," Jafar replied. "By beheading."

Jasmine felt her knees go weak. That poor boy—this was all her fault!

"How could you?" she whispered to Jafar. Then she turned and ran away, sobbing.

A few minutes later, she sat at the edge of the fountain in the palace gardens. Rajah gazed at her somberly.

"It's all my fault, Rajah," Jasmine said, hugging the tiger for comfort. She couldn't believe that the wonderful, lively, caring boy she had met was gone forever. And all because he had tried to help her.

"I didn't even know his name," she whispered.

PRINCE ALI

"Jafar, this is an outrage!" the Sultan cried. Jasmine had come to him, terribly upset, babbling something about a boy and a beheading and the grand vizier. After a while, he'd managed to figure out what it was she was sobbing about. "If it weren't for all your years of loyal service . . . but from now on, you're to discuss sentencing of prisoners with me—*before* they are beheaded!"

"I assure you, Your Highness, it won't happen again," Jafar replied.

The Sultan sighed with relief. Good—then, that

was settled. "Jasmine, Jafar," he said, taking one of each of their hands and bringing them together. "Now, let's put this whole messy business behind us."

"My most abject and humblest apologies to you as well, Princess," Jafar said to Jasmine.

Jasmine scowled in return. "At least some good will come of my being forced to marry," she declared. "When I am queen, I will have the power to get rid of *you*!"

With that, she turned and stormed away. How

dare Jafar think a simple apology would make up for what he had done? Yes, the sooner he was gone from the palace, the better. Of course, that didn't make her much happier about being forced to marry a man she didn't love. . . .

As she thought about that, there was a sudden commotion from outside the palace walls. Curious, Jasmine stepped out on the balcony of her quarters.

There was an enormous procession making its way through the streets of the city, headed toward the royal palace. At the front of the parade was a group of dancers in splendid, bejeweled attire. Next came an imposing regiment of armed guards followed by dozens of glamorously dressed servants and a menagerie of exotic animals. Musicians played trumpets, drums, tambourines, and flutes. An elephant draped in beautiful silks carried a magnificent canopied seat on its back. Upon the seat, a handsome young man dressed in white waved to the crowds that had gathered to see him pass.

"Make way for Prince Ali Ababwa!" someone shouted.

Another suitor, Jasmine thought with a sigh—does he really think he can win my heart with such a spectacle?

She had seen enough. Spinning on her heel, she went back inside. But she could still hear the music and the shouts of the spectators.

After a moment, her curiosity got the better of her. What would her father think of this latest suitor? After all, her birthday was only two days from now. . . .

Jasmine crept toward the throne room, listening to the muffled voices coming from within. She could hear her father giggling, sounding delighted, and Jafar muttering, sounding annoyed. She also heard a third voice—a strangely familiar one.

She peered into the room. Her father was clapping his hands happily. "Jasmine will like this one!" he cried.

Prince Ali Ababwa smiled. "And I'm pretty sure I'll like Princess Jasmine."

Jasmine frowned. No, the voice wasn't familiar, after all. She had never in her life heard anyone sound so pompous. She entered the throne room, but the trio didn't notice her.

"Your Highness, no," Jafar put in. "I must intercede—on Jasmine's behalf. This boy is no different from the others. What makes him think he is worthy of the princess?"

"Your Majesty, I am Prince Ali Ababwa!" the young man responded. "Just let her meet me! I will win your daughter."

This was too much! "How dare you!" Jasmine cried. "All of you! I am not a prize to be won!" Before the startled men could respond, she turned and stormed out.

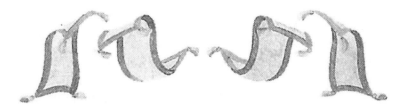

Later that evening, Jasmine sat in her room, wondering if she would ever be happy again. It was a beautiful night, clear and warm, with countless stars twinkling in the sky overhead. But Jasmine was in no mood to appreciate their beauty. Even Rajah's company couldn't cheer her up.

"Princess Jasmine." A voice reached her ears. It came from the balcony.

Jasmine blinked in surprise. Nobody could get to her balcony without passing through this very room. "Who's there?" she called suspiciously.

"It's me, Prince Ali Ababwa."

Jasmine frowned. However he had reached the balcony, she wasn't interested. "I do not want to see you," she retorted.

Rajah loped out toward the balcony. A moment later, Jasmine heard the prince babbling in fear. She smiled and went to the doorway to watch.

The young man had his turban in his hand, trying to shoo the huge tiger away. Without his turban, he looked . . . different. Almost familiar. Jasmine gazed at him thoughtfully.

"Wait," she said. "Do I know you? You remind me of someone I met in the marketplace."

"The marketplace?" Prince Ali repeated, quickly placing the turban back on his head. "Ha! I have servants who go to the marketplace for me. Why, I even have servants who go to the marketplace for my servants. So, it couldn't have been me you met."

Jasmine sighed. She should have known it was wishful thinking that had made this stuck-up prince look so much like that boy she had met. "No, I guess not," she murmured.

Meanwhile, the prince was giving her a nervous smile. "Um, Princess Jasmine," he said. "You're very . . . punctual."

Jasmine wondered if she had heard him right. "Punctual?"

"Uh—uh—beautiful!" the prince corrected quickly.

Jasmine sighed. All the other suitors had said the same thing. "I'm rich, too," she said, giving in to the temptation to tease him a little. "The daughter of a sultan."

"I know," Prince Ali said eagerly.

"A fine prize for any prince to marry," Jasmine went on.

"Uh, right," Prince Ali agreed uncertainly. "A prince like me."

Jasmine had had enough of this game. "Right—a

prince like you," she snapped. "And every other stuffed shirt, swaggering peacock I've met!" She waved a hand dismissively, suddenly wishing he would just disappear. "Just—jump off a balcony!"

"Uh, you're right," Prince Ali said quietly. "You aren't just some prize to be won. You should be free to make your own choice. I'll go now."

With that, he stepped off the edge of the balcony. Jasmine gasped. It was many stories to the hard ground below. He would be killed!

"No!" she cried.

"What?" he said, stopping . . . in midair!

"How are you doing that?" she asked, perplexed. She stepped forward as the prince floated upward. He was standing on a carpet!

"It's a magic carpet," he explained. "You don't want to go for a ride, do you?"

Jasmine hesitated. A magic carpet? She had heard stories of such things. And it would mean another chance to leave the confines of her golden cage. . . .

"Is it safe?" she asked uncertainly.

"Sure," Prince Ali replied. "Do you trust me?" he asked, offering his hand. She stared at him in amazement. Hadn't she already lived this moment?

"Yes!" she whispered, taking his hand.

The stars shone like diamonds as Jasmine settled down on the Magic Carpet. Prince Ali sat beside her. And then they were off!

The Magic Carpet swooped up, up, up, high into the warm night air. Jasmine hardly knew where to look first as they sped over the city. Below, she could see the winding, twisting streets; the crowded, colorful stalls of the marketplace; and the lights of the palace shining over it all.

Then they were leaving Agrabah. The carpet carried them over the desert, where caravans moved slowly over the sand, and herds of wild horses ran free. They passed over rivers, pyramids, cities, and oceans. Finally, they settled onto the roof of a strange building in a strange, far-off land. Below, in a square, people wearing dragon costumes danced and shouted. To Jasmine's amazement, colorful lights started exploding in the sky overhead— fireworks! She had never seen so many wonders in her life. She had never even imagined them!

"It's all so magical!" she exclaimed, leaning against Prince Ali's shoulder.

When she turned to look into his eyes, she saw something there—something warm, and true, and very, very familiar. Suddenly, she knew how she could find out if she was imagining things or not. . . .

"It's a shame Abu had to miss this," she commented casually.

The prince shrugged. "Nah, he hates fireworks.

He doesn't really like flying, either." Suddenly realizing what he'd said, he gulped. "Uh, um—oh, no!"

"You *are* the boy from the market!" Jasmine cried. "I knew it. Why did you lie to me? Who are you? Tell me the truth!"

"The truth?" Prince Ali looked nervous. "The truth is, I sometimes dress as a commoner to escape the pressures of palace life. But I really am a prince."

Jasmine's anger had already passed. She knew about those pressures herself—all too well. "Why didn't you just tell me?" she asked.

"Well, you know . . . royalty going out into the city in disguise—it sounds a little strange, don't you think?"

"Not *that* strange," Jasmine said. Suddenly tired of arguing, she leaned against him. So what if he had kept a secret? It didn't matter. He had told the truth now.

When the fireworks ended, the two of them climbed back onto the Magic Carpet and flew home. Jasmine couldn't remember the last time she had felt so happy.

Prince Ali brought her back to the balcony, helping her step down from the carpet. "Good night, my handsome prince," she said softly.

"Sleep well, Princess," Prince Ali replied, pulling her toward him for a sweet, good-night kiss.

THE MAGIC OF LOVE

"Oh, Rajah, it was such a wonderful night!" Jasmine cried as soon as she reached her room, with the warmth of Prince Ali's kiss still on her lips.

She sat down before her mirror and picked up a brush. As she brushed her hair, humming the love song Prince Ali had sang to her on their Magic Carpet ride, she thought back over every incredible moment of the evening with the prince. Prince Ali—her friend, her true love, her husband-to-be. Just a day before, she never would have believed

that everything could work out so perfectly.

Jasmine was beside herself with joy. Now she could fulfill her father's wishes, obey the law, and marry a prince by her sixteenth birthday. Prince Ali had arrived just in time to make everyone's dreams come true! Jasmine still could hardly believe how lucky she was. She had to be the luckiest—and happiest—girl in all of Agrabah. In fact, she was sure she had to be the happiest girl in all the world!

Her only regret was that her mother couldn't be there to share in her joy. If only she were still alive . . .

Jasmine wandered to the window and gazed up at the twinkling stars. "Oh, Mother," she whispered. "If you can hear me somehow, hear this. I'm in love! Your little girl has found true love at last. And with Prince Ali by my side, nothing will ever be able to make me unhappy again. . . ."

But there were a few things that Jasmine didn't know about her handsome prince. She didn't know that he was really the street rat Aladdin. He had only become a prince with the help of a genie in a magic lamp!

For Jafar had never had any intention of beheading the young man his guards had taken prisoner. At least, not until Aladdin had served his purpose . . .

Appearing to the boy as an old beggar, Jafar had helped Aladdin escape from the dungeon and find the Cave of Wonders. Once there, the old man had ordered Aladdin to find the lamp and bring it to him. After that, all the other treasures of the cave would be Jafar's for the taking.

Aladdin had agreed to the plan. Maybe if he discovered a cave full of untold riches, he could prove himself worthy of the beautiful princess who had stolen his heart! But his monkey companion couldn't stop himself from grabbing an enormous jewel. And as soon as Abu's paw touched it, the tiger-spirit awoke from its slumber. The walls of the cave had begun to quake, and the piles of gold coins melted into an endless flow of molten lava.

The only thing that had saved them was the Magic Carpet. It had whisked them through the inferno to the mouth of the cave where Jafar was waiting for the lamp. Suddenly, the cave's mouth had slammed shut, trapping Aladdin, Abu, and the Magic Carpet inside.

Luckily, Abu still had the lamp! He gave it to Aladdin who rubbed it, trying to read the inscription on its side. Seconds later, a huge, jolly blue genie had burst out of the lamp and offered Aladdin three wishes!

As soon as the Genie had used his magical powers to get everyone out of the cave, Aladdin had chosen his first wish: to become a prince so that he could woo the Sultan's daughter. And so the Genie had transformed him into Prince Ali Ababwa. . . .

Jasmine was still caught up in the magical evening she had shared with Prince Ali when her father arrived at her chamber. She smiled when she saw him, rushing to give him a hug. "Oh, Father! I am so happy!" she said, greeting him.

"You should be, Jasmine," the Sultan replied. "I have chosen a husband for you."

"What?" Her smile disappeared. For the first time, she noticed that the Sultan's eyes looked glazed and far away.

"You will marry Jafar," the Sultan went on.

Jasmine gasped in horror. What was her father talking about? She had chosen her suitor!

The grand vizier and his parrot, Iago, had followed the Sultan into the room. "You're speechless, I see," he said with a cruel laugh. "A fine quality in a wife."

"I'll never agree to marry you!" Jasmine cried. "Father, I choose Prince Ali!"

"Prince Ali

left," the grand vizier said with a wicked smile. He had ordered his guards to knock the boy unconscious and toss him into the deep sea.

"Better check your crystal ball again, Jafar," a new voice interrupted.

"Prince Ali!" Jasmine exclaimed in relief.

Aladdin was furious. It was only the Genie's magic that had saved him from Jafar's dastardly plans. Now, he meant to take care of the evil vizier once and for all. "Tell them the truth, Jafar," Aladdin demanded. "You tried to have me killed."

"What ridiculous nonsense," Jafar said, chuckling nervously.

"Your Highness," Aladdin said, striding toward Jafar and the Sultan, "Jafar has been controlling you with this." He grabbed the cobra staff and smashed it to the ground.

The Sultan immediately came out of his trance.
"What?" he sputtered in confusion. "Jafar? You
traitor!"

He called for the guards, but Jafar was too quick
for him. "This is not done yet," the vizier vowed,
disappearing in a cloud of smoke.

Aladdin hurried toward the princess. "Jasmine,
are you all right?"

"Oh, yes!" Jasmine cried. The two of them
embraced.

The Sultan was still muttering about Jafar's treachery. But suddenly, he noticed what was going on. "What? Can this be true?" he exclaimed. "My daughter has finally chosen a suitor? Ha-ha!" The Sultan was thrilled. "You two will be wed at once. And you'll be happy and prosperous, and then you, my boy, will become Sultan!"

He kept babbling on in his happiness, but Jasmine wasn't really paying attention anymore. She was too busy imagining the wonderful, blissful future that lay ahead.

Jafar's Triumph

"Try this one, Princess." Amina stepped forward, holding out a soft bundle of purple cloth. Jasmine took it, noting the fine quality of the silk.

"It's beautiful, Amina!" she exclaimed.

Hurrying over to her dressing area, Jasmine quickly slipped on the gown. It fit perfectly, of course—the palace tailors had been working feverishly all night. Jasmine spun around in a circle, admiring the way the folds of the skirt danced around her legs.

"Here, this was made to match." Amina handed the princess a headpiece. The large blue gemstone on it was a twin to the one on the waistband of the gown.

Jasmine carefully fixed the headpiece in place. She smiled at her nursemaid. "Oh, Amina," she said with a sigh. "How can one girl be so happy?"

Amina returned the smile. "No princess ever deserved happiness so much as you, Your Highness," she said kindly. "I knew on the day that you were born that you would be special. I'm so glad your prince has seen that, too."

"Prince Ali is the special one." Jasmine smiled, imagining what the prince would say when he saw her in this dress. Should she save it for the wedding ceremony later, or wear it now to hear her father officially announce his daughter's engagement?

Suddenly, she realized that it was time for the announcement. That made up her mind—she would wear the dress now.

Since the earliest hours of the morning, rumors of the upcoming royal wedding had been flying throughout Agrabah. Guests from neighboring kingdoms were already on their way, and the city had adorned itself for the festivities—banners, flags, and flowers were everywhere, and the air was filled with joyful music. An immense crowd had gathered in front of the palace, eager to get a look at the young groom who would one day be their sultan.

That same morning, Jasmine had sent two of her handmaidens to an alley near the marketplace to find the little house where Kerim lived. The princess had not forgotten the promise she'd made to her little friend—young Kerim and his family would be honored guests at her wedding to Prince Ali.

But for now, Jasmine's thoughts were not of Kerim, but of her handsome prince. She hadn't seen Prince Ali all morning—and the time for the announcement was here! Where could he be?

"People of Agrabah!" her father began from a balcony overlooking the town square. "My daughter has finally chosen a suitor!"

As he went on, Jasmine heard another voice, much closer. "Jasmine?"

"Prince Ali!" she cried, spinning around. "Where have you been?"

"Jasmine, there's something I have to tell you," Prince Ali began.

Jasmine was too excited to pay attention to what he was saying. "The whole kingdom has turned out for Father's announcement!" she cried.

"No, but Jasmine, listen to me, please . . . you don't understand. . . ." Prince Ali said desperately.

Was he getting stage fright at the idea of stepping out before the whole kingdom? Jasmine decided it was better not to give him too much time to worry about it. Besides, her father had just announced the prince's name.

"Good luck!" she whispered, pushing him out onto the balcony.

Nearby, Jafar was watching the celebration, too. The moment he was waiting for had arrived. With an evil gleam in his eyes, he picked up a humble-looking lamp. His sidekick, Iago, had

stolen it from under Aladdin's pillow without the boy's knowing. Now, Jafar would have his revenge!

He rubbed the lamp. The Genie emerged, expecting to see Aladdin, who still had one wish remaining. He gulped in surprise as Jafar laughed triumphantly. "I am your master now!" the vizier cried. "Genie, grant me my first wish: I wish to rule on high—as sultan!"

The Genie was horrified, but he had no choice. It was his duty to obey. Summoning up his magical powers, he stripped away the Sultan's crown, his jewels, even his royal clothes. The poor Sultan was standing there in only his underwear! Seconds later, Jafar had taken his place as ruler of the kingdom. Jasmine could only watch helplessly, while Prince Ali stared at the Genie in horror. "Genie, no!" he exclaimed.

The Genie's big blue face was mournful. "Sorry, kid," he said. "I've got a new master now."

It didn't take long for the Sultan to realize what was happening. "Jafar, you vile betrayer!" he cried.

Jafar smiled. "Finally, you will bow to me," he said with a hiss.

"We will never bow to you!" Jasmine cried defiantly.

Jafar seethed with anger. How dare she? "If you won't bow to a sultan," he said, "then you will cower before a sorcerer! Genie—my second wish. I wish to be the most powerful sorcerer in the world!"

Once again, the Genie had no choice but to do his bidding. Soon Jafar was a mighty sorcerer. He forced the Sultan and Jasmine to their knees with his magic powers. When Rajah tried to stop him, Jafar transformed the tiger into a helpless kitten. But still, Jafar had more tricks up his sleeve.

"Oh, Princess," he said slyly. "There's someone I'm dying to introduce you to."

With that, he changed Prince Ali back into plain old Aladdin. "He's nothing more than a worthless, lying street rat!"

"Ali!" the princess cried in shock as she realized her prince wasn't a prince at all.

"Or should we say—Aladdin?" Iago said,

revealing the boy's real name to Jasmine for the first time.

Before Aladdin could explain, Jafar had flung him into a high tower. Then the sorcerer sent the tower flying up and away—until it landed in an icy land far from Agrabah.

As she watched the tower disappear, Jasmine felt all her hopes for happiness vanish along with it.

THE ULTIMATE POWER

Jasmine couldn't believe what was happening. She watched helplessly as the evil Jafar changed her father into a puppet dressed in a silly jester outfit. He continuously teased and bullied the poor Sultan. It was too much for Jasmine to bear.

"Stop it!" Jasmine cried. "Jafar, leave him alone!"

"It pains me to see you reduced to this, Jasmine," Jafar said, pulling the princess closer to him by the iron chains he had shackled around her. The princess could tell that it angered Jafar that she wouldn't surrender to his power. The angrier he got,

the more it gave her resolve. She would show him that it took more than magical power to defeat her!

The only thing that made it difficult to go on was thinking about Ali—Aladdin—whatever his real name was. She had thought he was her handsome prince. Now that she knew he was really a street rat, did it change the way she felt about him? Her heart told her no. She thought back to the hideaway on the roof of that old abandoned house, then to the incredible Magic Carpet ride among the stars. Both had been special, because she'd shared them with the one she loved.

She was disappointed that Aladdin had lied to her, but she was starting to understand the reason why he had done so. And remembering his words as she had pushed him out on the balcony to be introduced to the people of Agrabah, she was certain he had been about to tell her the truth at last—even though he would have risked losing her. And that only made her love him all the more.

As Jafar forced the former Sultan to dance for his amusement, Amina crept up to Jasmine's side. "Princess," she whispered, "are you all right?"

"Oh, Amina!" Jasmine's eyes filled with tears. "None of us are all right as long as Jafar is in charge."

Amina stroked her shoulder. "Take courage, Princess," she whispered. "I have an idea. That dented old lamp—it is what gives the evil one his power, yes?"

"Yes, that's right," Jasmine said, glancing at the lamp, which was nestled on a cushion at Jafar's side. "We need to get that lamp away from him."

Amina nodded and smiled slyly.

Jasmine gazed at the maid curiously. "Amina, what are you thinking?" she asked.

"I will save you, Princess," Amina said. "If you will distract the evil one for but a moment, I will be able to take the lamp and bring it to you. Then you will have the power to defeat him!"

Jasmine gasped. "Amina, no! I can't let you do that," she said. "It's far too dangerous. What if Jafar sees you?"

Amina tried to protest, but Jasmine wouldn't listen. She had made up her mind. Jafar had already destroyed one of her loved ones—she wouldn't let him take another.

Amina crept away. Jasmine thought the maid had given up on her crazy plan. But a moment later, Iago pointed to the back of Jafar's chair, where a humble figure was cowering. "You, there—what do you think you're doing?"

With a gasp, Jasmine recognized the figure as Amina. Oh, no! Jasmine's heart sank as she realized her friend had put her own life at risk for her.

"No!" the princess cried as Jafar stood and raised his magic staff. "It's not her fault. It was all my idea!"

"Take her away!" Jafar ordered coldly pointing to the frightened Amina. "She will pay for her betrayal when I've decided upon a fitting punishment."

Guards grabbed Amina and dragged her off. Jasmine watched her go, helpless to do anything to save her friend. When would this nightmare end?

Meanwhile, Jafar's attention had returned to the princess. He forced her to feed him an apple and offer him sips of wine as she grimaced with shame. "A beautiful desert bloom such as yourself should be on the arm of the most powerful man in the world," Jafar said. With his dark eyes glittering madly, he held out a delicate crown of gold.

"Never!" Jasmine cried, throwing the rest of the wine in Jafar's face.

Jafar growled angrily. He was about to strike her when he had a better idea. "Genie," he said, "I have decided to make my final wish: I wish for Princess Jasmine to fall desperately in love with me!" Jasmine gasped in horror. But to her surprise, nothing happened.

That was because the Genie's powers had certain limits—he couldn't kill anyone, raise anyone from the dead, or cause anyone to fall in love with someone else. But Jafar didn't know that.

As Jasmine wondered what would happen next, her eyes suddenly widened with shock. She had just spotted Aladdin at the window!

Though Jasmine didn't know it, Aladdin, with the help of Abu and the Magic Carpet, had narrowly escaped from the cold mountain where the tower had landed. Now, he was back to try to save Agrabah—and the girl he loved.

Jasmine's heart filled with joy, but that feeling was soon replaced by terror. What if Jafar spotted Aladdin now? It would all be over.

She decided the only thing to do was distract him. "Jafar," she said in a soft, beguiling voice. "I never realized how incredibly handsome you are." Slowly, she placed Jafar's elegant gold crown on her head.

The Genie stared in shock, knowing that his

magic had had nothing to do with this odd transformation. But Jafar seemed pleased.

"That's better," he said with satisfaction. "Now, pussycat, tell me more about myself."

Jasmine wanted to shudder with disgust as he smiled at her. Instead, she forced herself to move toward him. "You're tall," she purred, "dark, well dressed. . . ." She was running out of words, so she started praising his eyebrows, his beard, and everything else she could think of. "You've stolen my heart," she finished.

"And the street rat?" Jafar asked.

Jasmine forced herself to keep her gaze on the vizier. But out of the corner of her eye, she could see Aladdin sneaking up toward the lamp.

"What street rat?" she replied smoothly.

Suddenly, Iago, who was struggling with Abu a few feet away, knocked over a fruit bowl. Jafar began to turn toward the sound and—Aladdin!

Seeing what was happening, Jasmine acted fast. She grabbed Jafar—and kissed him.

It was the most horrible thing she had ever had to do. Worse yet, it didn't work. Jafar pulled away and spotted Aladdin and his friends. "You!" he bellowed. "How many times do I have to kill you, boy?"

Before Jasmine knew what was happening, Jafar had trapped her in a giant hourglass. He also turned Abu into a toy monkey, and unraveled the Magic Carpet into a pile of threads. Now, Aladdin had to face the vizier's wrath alone.

"Aladdin!" Jasmine cried desperately.

All she could do was watch as Jafar sent guards, enchanted swords, and everything else he could muster up after the street rat. "Are you afraid to fight me yourself, you cowardly snake?" Aladdin shouted as he dodged Jafar's magical forces.

Jafar laughed, then transformed himself into a huge monstrous cobra. He wrapped Aladdin in his coils. "You little fool," Jafar said with a hiss. "You thought you could defeat the most powerful being on earth? Without the Genie, boy, you're nothing!"

Jasmine pounded against the glass, but it seemed hopeless. The sands of the hourglass were pouring down, burying her alive. Outside, she saw Jafar's coils tightening around Aladdin.

"The Genie!" Aladdin shouted suddenly. "The Genie has more power than you'll ever have. He gave you your power. He could take it away. Face it, Jafar. You're still just second-best."

Jafar hesitated. He had never looked at it that way before. "You're right," he murmured uncertainly. "His power does exceed my own . . . but not for long!" His evil snake eyes flashed with cunning as he realized that since Jasmine hadn't fallen in love with him, he had one more wish left. "Slave!"

he howled at the Genie, who was cowering nearby. "I make my third wish: I wish to be—an all-powerful genie!"

Jasmine was horrified. Aladdin had just given Jafar the ultimate power! How could anybody hope to stop him now?

As Jafar changed form again, this time from cobra to genie, Aladdin slipped free of his grasp. Grabbing a staff, he broke the hourglass, setting Jasmine free seconds before the sand had buried her completely.

Gasping for breath, Jasmine looked up at Jafar. He had become an awe-inspiring red genie.

"The power!" he cried. "The absolute power!"

"What have you done?" Jasmine asked Aladdin sadly.

Instead of looking worried, Aladdin smiled. "Trust me," he murmured. Then he stood and called out to Jafar. "Aren't you forgetting something?" he said. "You wanted to be a genie—you got it. And everything that goes with it."

At that moment, heavy iron chains appeared, clamping firmly onto Jafar's wrists. He stared in horror. An evil-looking black lamp appeared. Jafar felt himself being sucked toward it. He howled in protest, grabbing at Iago to try to stop himself. But seconds later, Jafar disappeared into the lamp.

The Genie rushed over to Aladdin. "Al, you little genius, you!" he cried.

Meanwhile, now that Jafar was gone, all of his magic spells were reversing. Rajah, Abu, and the Magic Carpet returned to their original forms. The Sultan's royal clothes and crown were back, too.

Jasmine sighed with relief. She watched as the Genie picked up Jafar's lamp. "Ten thousand years in the Cave of Wonders ought to chill him out," he announced. He flung the lamp toward the horizon, farther than the human eye could see.

At that, Jasmine laughed out loud. The night-mare was over!

ALADDIN'S THIRD WISH

On the palace balcony, Jasmine and Aladdin stood gazing at each other. Now that Jafar had been defeated, the palace was getting back to normal. The Sultan had immediately freed Amina, who was none the worse for wear. The servants were busy fixing all the damage Jafar had done. Now, Jasmine and Aladdin had found a quiet moment together, and the time had come to put all the lies behind them.

"Jasmine, I'm sorry I lied to you about being a prince," Aladdin said.

"I know why you did." Jasmine smiled at him. She knew that it hadn't been ambition or greed that had made him do it—he had done it out of love. That didn't make it right, but it made it easier to forgive.

"Well, I guess this is good-bye," Aladdin said sadly.

Jasmine couldn't answer for a moment. It just didn't seem fair—they loved each other. But the law said she had to marry a prince, and Aladdin wasn't a prince. She glanced at her father, who was standing nearby. He looked sad, too.

The Genie was looking on. "Al, no problem," he said. "You've still got one wish left. Just say the word and you're a prince again!"

"But Genie, what about your freedom?" Aladdin protested. He had promised to use his third and final wish to free the Genie from his life of servitude. After all the Genie had done for him, he didn't want to go back on his word.

"This is love," the Genie replied. "Al, you're not

going to find another girl like her in a million years!"

Aladdin turned and looked into Jasmine's eyes. The Genie was right—he would never, ever meet anyone else like her. "Jasmine, I do love you," he said, his heart heavy. "But I've got to stop pretending to be something I'm not."

"I understand," Jasmine whispered, feeling as though her heart would break. Part of her wished that Aladdin would change his mind. But she also knew he wouldn't be the person she loved if he turned his back on the Genie.

Aladdin took a deep breath.

"Genie, I wish for your freedom! You're free."

A powerful whirlwind swirled around the

surprised Genie. His iron cuffs broke open, and the lamp fell to the ground, its magic gone.

The Genie laughed in amazement. "I'm free!" he cried.

Jasmine smiled as she watched him holler with joy. She knew how precious freedom was. Even if she was still trapped in her golden cage, she was glad the Genie could enjoy his freedom.

The Genie swooped down to wrap Aladdin in a grateful hug. "No matter what anybody says, you'll always be a prince to me."

"That's right!" the Sultan spoke up suddenly. "You've certainly proved your worth as far as I'm concerned." He shook his head. "It's that law that's the real problem." Then his face broke into a smile. "Well, am I Sultan, or am I Sultan?" he exclaimed.

"From this day forth, the princess can marry whomever she deems worthy!"

Jasmine hardly dared to believe her ears. Had her father really done it? Maybe he *did* understand her—much better than she had ever imagined!

"Him!" she burst out joyfully, leaping into Aladdin's waiting arms. "I choose—I choose you, Aladdin!"

Aladdin smiled, holding her tight. "Call me Al," he said.

Jasmine closed her eyes as their lips met in a loving and meaningful kiss. And this time, she knew that nothing would stop them from living happily ever after.

THE STORY OF
ESMERALDA

THE LIFE OF A GYPSY

They say that Paris is the most modern of cities, full of modern people with modern ideas, where one can grow accustomed to seeing travelers from faraway places from all over the world. But no one is ever happy to see me. That's because I am a gypsy.

The life of a gypsy is difficult and dangerous. Most people believe that all gypsies are thieves. When they see us, mothers pull their children close for fear that we will spirit them away. People like to have us tell their future by reading their palms, but if they don't like what we tell them, they say that we're all witches, anyway. Nobody seems to understand that gypsies are just people. Just as is true of everyone else, there are good and bad among us.

The soldiers especially don't believe there can be any good in a gypsy. They think we are all bad, and cause us trouble whenever they can.

One night, as I was dancing on the street with my little goat, Djali, trying to earn a few coins for food, a pair of guards appeared.

"All right, gypsy," one of the men said with a sneer as he eyed my sack of coins. "Where did you get the money?"

"For your information, I earned it!" I told them.

"Gypsies don't earn money," the guard said.

His companion nodded. "They steal it," he added.

Now I was truly angry. How many times have I seen the soldiers rob gypsies of their money before tossing them out of the city or throwing them in prison? "You would know a lot about stealing!" I cried.

"Troublemaker, huh?" the first guard said with a growl, grabbing for my bag.

I wasn't going to let my money go without a fight. Those coins were the only way Djali and I would eat that day. I yanked the bag back. Djali did his part, butting and kicking the men. We managed to pull away and run.

"Come back here, gypsy!" yelled one of the guards.

Glancing back, I saw them running after us. Djali and I are quick, but the guards were big and strong, and the streets were crowded. For a moment, I was sure they would catch us.

Then, a white horse stepped between us and them. The guards crashed right into it. To my surprise, the horse sat down—right on the two men!

The horse's rider was tall, with a blond beard and handsome face. I'd noticed him watching me dance earlier.

"Oh, dear, I'm sorry," the man told the guards,

though he didn't sound sorry at all. "Naughty horse. Naughty."

One of the guards drew his sword. "I'll teach you a lesson, peasant!" he shouted.

At that moment, the man with the horse flipped back his cape. Beneath it, he wore the uniform of a captain of the army. He drew his own sword.

"You were saying, lieutenant?" he said to the guard pleasantly.

The guards fell all over themselves, apologizing to the captain, but I didn't stick around to hear it. It was time for Djali and me to disappear while we still had the chance.

We ran into an alley. Moments later, we were disguised as an old beggar, a cape covering the two of us. A hat sat before us on the street for people's offerings.

Before long, we heard the same two guards coming our way. This time they were shouting for people to move aside.

"You!" one of them shouted at a passerby. "Make way for the captain!"

"Make way!" the other echoed.

I peered out from under the cloak and saw a blond, bearded man striding along. He paused right in front of us. I gulped. Was he looking at us? Did he know we were in here?

If so, he didn't say a word. He merely dropped a few coins in our hat and moved on.

Whew! I was relieved. As soon as the men were out of sight, Djali and I ran in the other direction. However, I couldn't stop thinking about that captain. Had he helped me on purpose? I didn't know, but I soon decided it didn't really matter one way or the other. A smart gypsy never trusts a soldier.

When we were far enough away, I stopped to count our money. There wasn't nearly enough for a

meal, so Djali and I found another good spot and began to dance again.

Soon, a small crowd had gathered to watch us. I smiled as the little goat leaped about near me. Djali loves to dance just as much as I do. Looking at him now, one would never guess at his sad start in life.

When I was just a little girl, my cousin Marco showed me an orchard he'd found. He wanted us to go in and pick fruit to eat.

"That's stealing," I told him.

He shook his head. "Look, cousin," he said. "There are so many pears on those trees that they're falling to the ground and rotting." He smiled at me. "We'll only take the ones that have already fallen. What's the harm in that?"

I hesitated. The plan still made me nervous. But I was hungry, and the sweet smell of ripe pears drifted toward me on the breeze.

Finally, I nodded. "All right," I agreed. "But we can only take the ones that have fallen."

We hurried in among the trees, watching nervously for the farmer. I started gathering the fallen pears, cradling them in my skirt.

Then I noticed Marco climbing one of the trees. "Hey, what are you doing?" I called to him.

"Don't worry," he said as he plucked a perfect, ripe pear from a branch. "This one was about to fall."

Before I could answer, there was an angry shout. Glancing over my shoulder, I saw a man rushing toward us, dragging a sad-looking young goat behind him on a rope.

"Look out!" I shouted.

Marco swung down from the tree. "Run!" he cried.

I started to do as he said, but my foot got caught on a tree root. I fell, spilling all the pears I had gathered. Seconds later, the farmer was towering over me.

"Gypsies!" he shouted. "I should have known!" He grabbed me by the arm and pulled me to my feet. Then he turned to scowl at the little goat. "They steal almost as much of my best fruit as you, worthless beast. I should toss the two of you into the river!"

"Please, sir!" I cried, trying to pull away. Marco had disappeared, leaving me alone. "We didn't mean any harm."

"No harm?" the farmer yelled. "You call stealing my property no harm? I'll show you harm, you little thief!"

He pulled back his hand as if to strike me. But before he could do so, he let out a yelp and leaped forward, dropping my arm and grabbing his own backside. Surprised, I saw the little goat standing there. He had just butted the nasty farmer!

"Run!" I called to the goat, suddenly hopeful again.

This time I didn't trip. I ran as fast as I could, jumping over the stone wall at the edge of the orchard. The little goat leaped right beside me, then stopped short with a bleat.

"What's wrong?" I asked, spinning around.

I saw that the rope around the goat's neck had gotten caught between two of the stones. The frightened animal yanked and twisted, trying with all his might to get free, but the rope was stuck fast.

All of a sudden, there was a shout. It was the farmer. He was coming after us—fast!

I gulped. If I ran now, I would escape the farmer's wrath, for sure. But that would mean leaving behind the goat that had helped me.

No, I couldn't do it. Instead, I raced back toward the stone wall. It only took a few seconds to free the goat from the rope, but that was almost enough time for the farmer to catch up to us.

"You go that way," I said to the goat, pointing to the left. "I'll go this way. He can't chase us both!"

The goat seemed to understand. We ran off in opposite directions, leaving the farmer cursing behind us. Once we were sure we'd lost him, we found each other again by the river. And brave little Djali has been my constant companion ever since.

THE FESTIVAL OF FOOLS

I made more money than usual dancing that day. The people of Paris were in a good and generous mood. That was probably because it was a festival day—soon the Festival of Fools would begin. It was a day for laughter, pranks, celebration, and fun. A day when all of Paris seemed to turn upside down and inside out.

Along with everyone else in Paris, I hurried to the main square in front of Notre Dame cathedral to join in the fun. Clopin, the leader of the gypsies, was already there when I arrived, leading the crowd in song and dance. Everyone was dressed up, and many wore masks. Some of these masks were beautiful, others were funny, while still others were hideous or frightening.

Some people tottered along on stilts, while others dragged small children by the hand. On a tightrope strung high above the square, a gypsy I knew thrilled everyone with his daring tricks. Musicians played cheerful music on the huge stage set up for the occasion, while many members of the audience danced and sang along. Altogether, it was a wonderful, busy, noisy, crowded, exciting scene.

Soon it would be my turn to dance, so I hurried into a gypsy tent to change my clothes. As I pulled on a robe, I heard a commotion behind me.

"Hey!" I cried, startled.

When I turned around, I saw that someone had stumbled into my tent and tripped over a stool. Djali was staring at him suspiciously, but I wasn't really nervous. I always had my dagger with me in case of emergencies. My cousin, Marco, gave it to me long ago—just after that trip to the orchard, in fact.

The stranger was wearing a hood, so it was hard to see his face. But it looked as though he was also wearing a mask. I suspected he was just a festivalgoer who had enjoyed a little too much wine.

"Are you all right?" I asked, bending over him.

"I—I didn't mean to," he said with a gasp, pulling his hood still lower. "I'm sorry."

His voice was soft and sounded kind. "Well, you're not hurt, are you?" I asked him. "Here, let's see."

I made a move to pull back his hood. He tried to edge away, but I was too quick for him. Soon his mask was revealed—a scary and hideous mask. Mismatched eyes bulged above a misshapen nose, and I saw that a humped back was part of the costume as well. The mask was so lifelike that it was hard to see where it ended and where the man's skin began.

A quick look showed that he was fine. "Just try to be a little more careful," I told him with a chuckle.

"I—I will," he whispered. Then he hurried out through the tent flap.

"By the way," I called after him—"great mask!"

After that, I had to hurry to get ready. I heard Clopin singing out my introduction. I smiled as he referred to me as "the finest girl in France." Straightening my skirt, I vowed to live up to his words by dancing my best.

I stepped forward as Clopin finished the introduction. "Dance, la Esmeralda, dance!" he cried.

Then he flung down a handful of colorful powder on the stage. There was a puff of red smoke, and when it cleared, Clopin was gone and I was standing in his place.

I smiled as the crowd roared its approval.

Then I began my dance. It was easy to lose myself in the movement, but I had learned long ago to stay alert. That was the only way to avoid being captured by soldiers.

Today, I had little worry about that. But I did

notice that Judge Claude Frollo was sitting in a special viewing stand in the audience. Even though he was a good distance away, I still felt a shudder of fear. Judge Frollo had long ago declared himself the mortal enemy of all gypsies. He was determined to rid Paris of us entirely if he could. It was by his orders that the guards harassed us, and at his hands that my mother, my father, and many other friends and relatives had disappeared.

However, I would never let Frollo know that he scared me. Instead, I danced toward him. As I approached, I saw another familiar face at his side—it was the captain from earlier! I was surprised and disappointed. It seemed that I had been right not to trust the handsome soldier. He was Frollo's new Captain of the Guard, and that meant he was my enemy.

Frollo's somber face grew darker as I approached him, dancing and twirling to the beat of the music. I

leaped across to the viewing
stand and landed right in
front of him. Leaning
toward him, I wrapped my
scarf around his neck to the
howls of the crowd. Frollo
scowled at me and yanked the scarf free as I danced
away.

When I returned to the stage, I noticed the
masked fellow who had stumbled into my tent,
watching at the edge of the crowd. I winked at him,
which made him pull the hood over his face. I
almost laughed out loud. He was a shy one!

I continued dancing. By the time I finished, the
audience was in a frenzy. I could tell that Clopin
was pleased as he leaped past me to introduce the
next bit of entertainment—it was time to crown the
King of Fools!

This was one of the highlights of the celebration.
The crowd always chose the most horrible, gruesome,
frightening face in Paris to be king for the day. That

was why people worked so hard on their masks—everyone wanted the chance to compete for the crown!

As I listened to Clopin explaining the contest to the crowd, I spotted my masked friend from before. Perfect! I thought. His mask was so hideous and so real that he was sure to win!

I reached down and grabbed my friend by the hand, pulling him up onstage. A number of other people in masks had already gathered on the stage, and I pushed him out among them.

Then, as Clopin sang to the crowd, urging them to vote with their voices, I began pulling off the contestants' masks.

First, I pulled off the mask of a man wearing a horse costume. He grunted and made an ugly face. But it wasn't enough for the crowd. They booed and jeered, and Djali butted the man off the stage.

I moved on to the next contestant, and the next, but the result was always the same. None of the faces was ugly enough for the audience.

Finally, I came to my friend from the tent. I

reached up, preparing to grab his mask. But instead of soft fabric or hide, my fingers felt only human skin. I stepped back in shock.

"That's no mask!" a man in the crowd shouted.

"It's his face!" a woman's voice added, sounding as shocked as I felt.

There were more murmurs and shouts. "He's hideous!" someone cried.

"It's the bell ringer from Notre Dame!" someone else called out.

Meanwhile, the man clapped his hands over his face. "Oh," he moaned. "Oh, oh!"

He was terrified and humiliated. While I still felt horrified at his appearance, I also felt guilty. It was my fault he was up here—I had exposed him to the ridicule of the crowd.

Meanwhile, Clopin took advantage of the uproar. "Ladies and gentlemen, don't panic," he cried. "We asked for the ugliest face in Paris, and here he is! Quasimodo, the Hunchback of Notre Dame!"

With that, the cries of horror turned to laughter. Several people leaped up onto the stage and lifted Quasimodo to their shoulders. They carried him to a litter and then hoisted him into the air.

Now I knew who the unfortunate man with the twisted face was. I had heard tales of the bell ringer who lived high atop the Cathedral of Notre Dame, ringing the bells at the appointed times, never coming out into the city. People said he was a ward of Judge Frollo, that the judge had saved the infant Quasimodo from gypsies.

I watched as the litter was carried all around the square, the crowd singing and shouting the new King of Fools' praises. At first Quasimodo looked nervous, but soon he relaxed. After a few minutes, he even seemed to be enjoying himself. He smiled and waved as the enormous crowd cheered him on.

I felt relieved as I wandered toward the tent. Perhaps I hadn't done him a bad turn, after all.

A few minutes later, as I glanced out of the tent, I saw that Quasimodo was being returned to the stage. I smiled as an old lady tossed him a bouquet of flowers. Others were throwing colorful confetti, which rained down around him. Quasimodo was smiling, seeming overwhelmed but pleased by the attention.

Then, an overripe tomato flew threw the air, landing on Quasimodo's face. "Long live the king!" someone jeered from the crowd.

I gasped in horror. More fruits and vegetables were already raining down on Quasimodo as others caught on to the cruel joke. Quasimodo tried to escape, but his foot slipped on a slimy bit of tomato. He fell to his knees as the crowd shouted with laughter. A couple of men slipped ropes around him, trapping him in place.

"Where are you going, hunchback?" someone shouted.

Quasimodo had nowhere to turn and no way to escape. I saw him glance at Judge Frollo, who was watching the whole scene from the viewing platform. The captain looked concerned, but Frollo's face was impassive. He made no move to help as the crowd continued jeering and pelting Quasimodo with anything the people could find—not only fruits and vegetables but stones as well.

I couldn't take it anymore. I leaped back onto the stage. "I'm sorry," I whispered to the miserable Quasimodo. "This wasn't supposed to happen." I wiped his face with my scarf.

Then, I turned to face the crowd. They had stopped throwing things when I got in the way. But they were still howling with awful, uncontrollable mirth. Meanwhile, Frollo was scowling at me.

"You!" he said. "Gypsy girl. Get down at once!"

I kneeled beside Quasimodo. "Yes, Your Honor," I told the judge. "Just as soon as I free this poor creature."

"I forbid it!" Frollo shouted furiously.

I had no idea why the judge would wish this humiliation on one who was supposed to be his ward. But I didn't care what his reasons were. Surely, they were no better than the reasons why he sent his soldiers after the gypsies. It only took a second to cut the ropes with my dagger.

"How dare you defy me?" Frollo hissed.

I stood and faced him. "You mistreat this poor boy the same way you mistreat my people!" I cried. "You speak of justice, yet you are cruel to those most in need of your help!"

"Silence!" Frollo roared.

I refused to heed him. "Justice!" I shouted in return, raising my fist in the air.

Frollo's face was pinched with rage. "Mark my words, gypsy," he told me. "You will pay for this insolence!"

"Then, it appears we've crowned the wrong fool," I taunted him. "The only fool I see is you!" I flung Quasimodo's "crown" at the judge and then leaped offstage into the crowd.

I was lucky the square was so crowded. Even though I could hear Frollo ordering his men to seize and arrest me, I knew I would be able to escape— this time, at least.

But I also knew I'd better stay out of Frollo's sight from now on. After seeing how he had treated his ward, Quasimodo, I didn't want to imagine what he would do if he ever caught me.

FRIEND OR FOE?

It was cool and dark inside the cathedral, where I stopped for refuge a short while later. I knew I would be safe there for the moment. Even Frollo wouldn't dare seize anyone inside the church. Such actions were strictly forbidden—the cathedral was a place of shelter for those in need.

Breathing in the scents of burning candles and incense, I wondered just what had happened. It surely had not been wise to provoke the most powerful, most feared man in Paris. But what else could I have done? I couldn't stand by and watch as he allowed poor Quasimodo to be mistreated.

As I thought about that, wondering why the bell ringer had emerged from his tower after all this time, I suddenly became aware of someone creeping up behind me. Acting on instinct, I whirled around. A second later, my pursuer was on the ground, with my hand holding his own sword at his throat.

To my amazement, it was the Captain of the Guard. "You!" I cried, realizing that my escape must not have been quite as clever as I had thought. Perhaps the soldier had recognized my beggar's outfit, which I had used to slip away from the crowd and enter here.

"Easy, easy!" the man said nervously. "Uh, I—I just shaved this morning."

I almost smiled at his quip. But I didn't pull back the sword. "Oh, really?" I retorted. "You missed a spot."

"All right, all right," the man said. "Just calm down. Give me a chance to apologize."

I was surprised. "For what?" I asked.

Instead of replying, the soldier suddenly grabbed the sword out of my hands. With a quick toss, he sent me tumbling to the floor.

"That, for example," he said.

I was furious—and nervous. Fortunately, he didn't seem anxious to use the sword against me. "Are you always this charming?" I snapped. "Or am I just lucky?"

As I spoke, I grabbed a candelabrum and swung it at him. He blocked the blow easily with his sword. Obviously, he was much quicker than most.

Still, I wasn't about to give up. I was sure Frollo had sent him for me. I continued swinging the candelabrum at him. Soon, he was panting with the effort of avoiding my blows.

"You fight almost as well as a man," he said.

"Funny," I replied. "I was going to say the same thing about you!"

Finally, I landed a blow with the candelabrum, striking him on the jaw. Djali had been hiding since the man's appearance, but now he leaped forward to help, butting the soldier in the stomach.

The man grunted. "Didn't know you had a kid," he joked weakly. I was about to strike him again, but something stopped me. For a soldier, this man didn't seem to be trying very hard to hurt me. "Uh, permit me," he said as I stared down at him. "I'm Phoebus. It means 'sun god.'"

I blinked. It was a very strange name for a soldier—or for anyone.

"And you are?" Phoebus prompted.

Suddenly suspicious again, I glared at him. "Is this an interrogation?"

He put away his sword. "It's called an introduction," he replied with a smile.

"You're not arresting me?" I asked.

"Not as long as you're in here," he said. "I can't."

I was a bit surprised. When I'd seen him behind me, I had been sure he was going to defy the sanctuary of the church and grab me. It wouldn't be unlike Frollo's men to do just that.

"Huh?" I said. "You're not at all like the other soldiers."

"Thank you." Phoebus smiled.

When he asked my name again, I decided there was no harm in answering. "Esmeralda," I said.

"Beautiful," he responded. "Much better than Phoebus, anyway."

At that moment, a new voice interrupted. "Good work, captain. Now arrest her."

I gasped. It was Frollo! He was standing with a small group of soldiers, blocking the doorway. Djali cowered behind me as I stared at them in horror.

"Claim sanctuary!" Phoebus whispered behind me. "Say it!"

"You tricked me!" I said accusingly. What was I thinking? He worked for Frollo—our greatest enemy!

Phoebus turned to address Frollo. "I'm sorry, sir," he said. "She claimed sanctuary. There's nothing I can do."

Frollo scowled. "Then drag her outside and—"

"Frollo!" another voice broke in. "You will not touch her."

This time it was the Archdeacon, the head of the cathedral. He glared at Frollo, then glanced toward me. "Don't worry," he said. "Minister Frollo learned years ago to respect the sanctity of the church."

The Archdeacon ordered the soldiers out, and I thought I was safe. But as Frollo turned to leave, he grabbed me by the arm.

"You think you've outwitted me," he said, hissing in my ear. "But I am a patient man. And gypsies don't do well inside stone walls. You've chosen a magnificent prison, but it is a prison, nonetheless." He sneered as he released me and walked toward the door. "Set one foot outside, and you're mine!"

Meeting a Monster

I slumped to the floor. It was true—I was trapped! There was only a handful of exits leading out of the cathedral. Frollo could easily order his soldiers to guard all of them. There was no escape!

Still, I couldn't just give up. "If Frollo thinks he can keep us here, he's wrong!" I said fiercely.

The Archdeacon glanced at me. "Don't act rashly, my child," he said quietly. "You created quite a stir at the festival. It would be unwise to arouse Frollo's anger further."

"You saw what he did out there," I reminded the priest. "Letting the crowd torture that poor boy!"

The Archdeacon shook his head sadly. "You can't right all the wrongs of this world by yourself."

That was true enough, I realized. But did that mean I shouldn't even try? That didn't seem right. Quasimodo had been all alone up there, an outcast from society, just because he looked different from most people. I knew exactly how that felt—I was an outcast, too, only because I was a gypsy.

As I stared at the statues and stained-glass windows in the cathedral, wondering what to do, I heard someone speak.

"You! Bell ringer! What are you doing down here?"

I turned and saw a churchgoer glaring angrily toward the stairs. When I followed his gaze, I saw Quasimodo cowering there.

"Haven't you caused enough trouble already?" the churchgoer asked angrily.

Quasimodo turned and started to hurry away.

But I stepped forward. "Wait," I called to him. "I want to talk to you."

Before the sentence was out of my mouth, Quasimodo had disappeared up the stairs. I followed, running up the staircase with Djali at my heels.

I caught up to him on a high parapet wall. Several stone gargoyles guarded the place, which offered a beautiful view of the city below.

"Here you are!" I exclaimed, panting a bit from the chase. "I was afraid I'd lost you."

Quasimodo looked nervous. "Yes," he said. "Uh, I have chores to do. I-i-it was nice seeing you again."

"Wait!" I cried again. I wasn't going to let him get away without his hearing what I wanted to say. "I'm really sorry about this afternoon. I had no idea who you were. I would never have pulled you up on the stage."

He was still trying to escape, climbing up a ladder leading to yet another level. I followed him again and emerged into a sort of apartment high above the cathedral. It held a few bits of furniture, including a table with a tiny model version of the city of Paris. The great iron bells of Notre Dame were visible nearby.

I stared around curiously. "What is this place?"

"This is where I live," Quasimodo answered shyly.

I stepped forward for a better look at the table. "Did you make all these things yourself?" I was amazed at the detail in the models—tiny buildings, tiny animals, tiny everything! "This is beautiful! If I could do this, you wouldn't find me dancing in the street for coins!"

"But you're a wonderful dancer!" Quasimodo protested.

"Well, it keeps bread on the table." I noticed that part of the city model was covered by a cloth. I reached for it, wondering what was underneath: "What's this?"

"Oh, no, please!" Quasimodo cried. "I—I'm not finished. I still have to paint them."

But I had already seen the little human figures underneath. I even recognized some of them. "It's the blacksmith!" I cried with delight. "And the baker! You're a surprising person, Quasimodo. Not to mention, lucky. All this room to yourself?" I could hardly imagine it. I had never even had a corner of a room all to myself in my life!

Quasimodo shrugged. "Well, it's not just me. There's the gargoyles, and of course the bells. Would you like to see them?" he asked.

"Yes, of course!" I could tell the bells were special to him. "Wouldn't we, Djali?" I added warningly to the goat, who was about to chew on one of the tiny figurines.

Quasimodo took us on a tour of the many bells of Notre Dame. He had names for each of them—Little Sophia, Jeanne-Marie, Big Marie, and many more. After that, he showed us the view over Paris from the bell tower. It was breathtaking—the city looked beautiful and peaceful from high up there.

"I could stay up here forever!" I exclaimed.

"Y-you could, you know," Quasimodo suggested.

I shook my head. "No, I couldn't. Gypsies don't do well inside stone walls."

"But you're not like the other gypsies. They are—evil!" he exclaimed.

I frowned, surprised that such a belief would come out of such a gentle soul. "Who told you that?" I demanded.

"My master, Frollo," Quasimodo said. "He raised me. He took me in when no one else would. I am a monster, you know."

"He told you that?" I asked. I should have guessed. Only an evil man like Frollo could fill Quasimodo's mind with such nasty ideas.

Quasimodo seemed sad. "Just look at me," he murmured.

Knowing that I had caused him still more pain earlier at the festival, I wanted to help him feel a little better if I could. "Give me your hand," I said.

Then I pretended to read his palm. I pointed out his long lifeline and another line indicating his shyness. Then I stared more closely.

"Hmm, that's funny," I said. "I don't see any monster lines. Not a single one." I held out my own hand toward him. "Now you look at me. Do you think *I'm* evil?"

"No!" he cried immediately. "You are kind and good and . . . and . . ."

"And a gypsy," I finished for him. "And maybe Frollo's wrong about both of us."

He seemed willing to think about that. In the

meantime, my mind was returning to my own problems. How was I going to escape? There just didn't seem to be a way.

Quasimodo guessed what I was thinking. "You helped me," he said. "Now I will help you."

"But there's no way out," I said sadly. "There are soldiers at every door."

"We won't use a door," Quasimodo said.

"You mean, climb down?" I asked in amazement, glancing over the wall at the ground far, far below.

"Sure," Quasimodo said. He gestured toward Djali. "You carry him," he told me, "and I carry you."

It hardly seemed possible. But I was willing to try anything to escape the prison Frollo had made of the cathedral. "Come on, Djali," I said.

The little goat jumped into my arms, and then Quasimodo lifted us up. His arms were surprisingly strong.

"Don't be afraid," he told me.

"I am not afraid," I replied, though that wasn't entirely true.

Quasimodo grabbed a gargoyle for support, then swung over the wall. We were up so high that the ground seemed farther away than ever! But the bell ringer didn't hesitate. He swung around the side of the tower, confident and sure.

Soon we were making our way down the outside walls of the cathedral. I hardly dared to watch. At one point, a bit of the roof broke off, and we slid

partway down. But Quasimodo managed to grab a part of a buttress before the roof piece flew off into space. Moments later, we were safely on the ground, out of sight of the guards.

"I hope I didn't scare you," Quasimodo whispered.

"Not for an instant." I lied gratefully. Suddenly, I had a wonderful idea. "Come with me," I told him.

"What?" he asked in disbelief.

"To the Court of Miracles," I explained. That was the name of the gypsy hideaway deep beneath the city. Everyone knew of its existence, though we gypsies were the only ones who knew how to get there. "Leave this place."

"Oh, no." Quasimodo shook his head. "I'm never going back out there again. You saw what happened today. This is where I belong."

"All right," I said, seeing that his mind was made up. "Then I'll come to see you." Still, I felt I owed the bell ringer some token of my thanks. He had risked everything for me.

Then I had another idea. I reached up and

removed the necklace I was wearing, with its elabo-
rate woven amulet. I handed it to him.

"If *you* ever need sanctuary," I told him, "this will
show you the way." Then I quoted the rhyme I'd
been taught as a child. "When you wear this woven
band, you hold the city in your hand."

Djali was getting restless, and I knew it was time

to leave before the guards heard us. While Quasimodo tucked the amulet beneath his shirt, the little goat and I dashed off into the darkness.

As I rounded a corner heading away from the cathedral, I heard a soft whistle. I recognized my cousin's signal. "Marco!" I cried, spying him in a doorway.

"How did you manage to get out of the cathedral?" he asked me in amazement.

"It would take too long to explain," I answered, glancing around nervously at the sound of the guards doing their rounds nearby. We stayed still and silent until we were sure they had passed.

"I know a safe place where you can spend the night," Marco said. "Not our people, but they're good, and we can trust them."

I nodded without another word.

My cousin took me to the home of a miller just outside the city. One of the servants led us to the barn, where we could spend the night.

I settled into the pile of straw with relief. It had been a very long day. With my head resting on Djali's soft belly, I fell asleep almost immediately.

FLAMES OF ANGER

The next morning, we slipped away early. Marco went in one direction, and Djali and I in another. We had only walked a short distance from the mill when I heard shouts from somewhere behind us.

"What was that?" I murmured. The nervous feeling in my stomach told me it could not be good news.

I sneaked back through the fields for a look. To my horror, I saw soldiers wandering around in the yard outside the mill where I'd stayed the night before. Were they there looking for me? How had they known?

Pulling the beggar disguise over myself and the goat, I watched from a distance. When no one seemed to notice me, I moved a little closer, weaving in among the crowd of onlookers, wanting to hear what was going on.

"Poor miller," a woman said, shaking her head as she watched the soldiers stomp in and out of the mill. "He's never harmed anyone."

A man nodded his agreement. "Frollo's gone mad," he commented.

Just then, I spotted Frollo himself. He was questioning the miller. "Have you been harboring gypsies?" he demanded.

"Our home is always open to the weary traveler," the miller responded. "Have mercy, my lord. I assure you, we know nothing of these gypsies."

Frollo's soldiers exited the mill. I saw that Phoebus was among them. Then Frollo himself shut the door and slid a spear through the door latch, locking the miller and his family inside.

The judge looked at Phoebus, who was holding a torch. "Burn it," he ordered.

I gasped in shock. Phoebus looked startled. "What?" he exclaimed.

"Until it smolders," Frollo added.

"With all due respect, sir, I was not trained to murder the innocent," Phoebus said.

Frollo glared at him. "But you *were* trained to follow orders."

Phoebus stared back, and for a moment I feared he would do as Frollo had commanded. For some reason, this seemed more terrible than anything else that was happening.

But then, the captain took his torch and

dropped it into a bucket of water. The flame was extinguished with a sizzle of steam.

"Insolent coward!" Frollo shouted in anger. And with that, he grabbed a torch from another soldier and lit the mill house ablaze himself!

I was certain that the miller and his family were doomed. And it was all because of me!

But all of a sudden, Phoebus leaped forward. He broke a window and rescued the family. I gasped in amazement. Maybe he really *was* different from the other soldiers!

Then I gasped again, this time in horror. One of Frollo's other soldiers had just sneaked up and

knocked Phoebus down with his sword! Frollo himself was riding toward him on his horse.

"The sentence for insubordination," Frollo announced coldly, staring down at Phoebus, "is death. Such a pity. You threw away a promising career."

Phoebus glared at Frollo, but I didn't wait to see what he would do. Grabbing a stone, I ran forward and flung it at Frollo's horse, using my scarf as a slingshot.

My aim was good. The stone struck the horse on its hindquarters, startling it. It reared and bucked, throwing Frollo to the ground.

Phoebus sprang to his feet. Pushing away the confused soldiers, he leaped onto Frollo's horse.

"Get him!" Frollo screamed as Phoebus rode off. "And don't hit my horse!"

The other men raced after Phoebus. Arrows flew through the air all around him. Phoebus galloped across a bridge, heading for the woods. But just when I hoped that he might be able to escape,

an arrow struck him in the back. He tumbled off the horse and over the edge of the bridge into the river.

I ran toward the water, with Djali following close behind. Frollo didn't see me—he was looking down into the river. "Don't waste your arrows," he told his men as they prepared to shoot again. "Let the traitor rot in his watery grave.

"Now find the girl!" he added. "If you have to burn the city to the ground, so be it!"

He was talking about me. I should have run for the woods myself, but I couldn't leave Phoebus behind. Especially after he had been so noble and brave. I had to see if he was still alive.

As soon as the soldiers were gone, I dove into the river. Phoebus was floating facedown, and for a moment I almost gave up hope.

But I had to try to rescue him. I swam toward him, and as soon as I touched him, I realized he

was still alive. The wound from the arrow was
bleeding a little, but it didn't look too bad up
close.

Hooking my arm under his, I held him tightly
and swam for the shore.

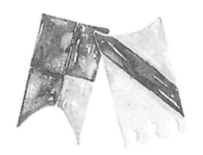

THE COURT OF MIRACLES

"Quasimodo?" I called, panting as I reached the top of the staircase leading to the bell tower. I had never been so tired in all my life. It had taken everything I had to get Phoebus this far. Luckily, a friend, a gypsy named Homer, had found me struggling to carry the soldier. After hearing the tale, he had offered to help me sneak the injured man back into the cathedral. I think he liked the idea of putting one over on the evil Frollo.

"Esmeralda?" Quasimodo's soft voice replied to my call. He sounded surprised.

It was no wonder he sounded that way. Half of Paris was on fire—I could hardly believe that Frollo was willing to destroy so much just to find me!

"You're all right!" Quasimodo cried, hugging me. "I knew you'd come back."

I was glad to see him. But this was no time for pleasantries. "You've done so much for me already, my friend. But I must ask for your help one more time," I begged.

"Yes," he said immediately. "Anything."

I was relieved. At my signal, Homer carried Phoebus into the room.

"This is Phoebus," I told Quasimodo. "He's wounded and a fugitive like me. He can't go on much longer. I knew he'd be safe here. Please, can you hide him?"

Quasimodo gestured for Homer to follow. "This way."

Soon Phoebus was resting in Quasimodo's own bed. The wounded soldier had been unconscious for most of the journey, but now he opened his eyes and looked up at me.

"Esmeralda," he said weakly.

I shushed him. "You'll hide here until you're strong enough to move."

Quasimodo brought a bottle of wine, which I used to clean Phoebus's wound. I could tell it was very painful, but he gritted his teeth and told jokes while I did my doctoring.

As I was stitching the wound, Phoebus let out a

groan. "Why is it, whenever we meet, I end up bleeding?" he quipped.

"You're lucky," I said as I bit the thread to cut it. "That arrow almost pierced your heart."

He caught my hand, holding it against his chest. "I'm not so sure it didn't," he replied.

I stared down at him. He gazed back at me. For a moment, I found myself lost in his eyes. He pulled me closer, and our lips met in a sweet kiss.

The tender moment was interrupted when I heard Djali bleat with fright out on the balcony. A moment later, Quasimodo called to me, sounding frantic.

"Frollo's coming!" he cried. "You must leave!"

He led me to a different staircase. Homer had already disappeared. I paused before running down, touching Quasimodo's hand.

"Be careful, my friend," I told him. "Promise you won't let anything happen to him."

"I promise," Quasimodo replied.

Soon Djali and I were slipping through the streets of Paris. The air was full of smoke, and a reddish glare lit up the night. It was horrible. There was only one place I could go to feel safe.

A little while later, I was pushing back the lid of a tomb in the cemetery. Stairs led down through the tomb into the old catacombs beneath the city. That was the place the gypsies called the Court of Miracles, the one safe hideaway Frollo had never been able to discover and destroy.

When I reached the main living area, Clopin was waiting there for me. "Welcome back, la Esmeralda," he said without smiling. "I suppose you know you are the reason for this fireworks display. Frollo is burning down half of Paris, and every gypsy that he sees is a dead man."

"I am not the reason," I said, correcting him. "Frollo himself is the one who has gone crazy." I shrugged. "He has always hated us. I am only today's convenient excuse." I sat down at the table and cut myself a piece of bread.

Clopin sighed. "I suppose you're right. But what do reasons matter? We are all in danger. As long as Frollo lives, we gypsies can have only half a life." He took the bread knife and angrily stabbed it into the wooden table.

As he left the room, I pulled the knife free. Despite what I had told Clopin, I did feel guilty for having set off Frollo's rage. But what else could I have done? Let Quasimodo be tormented for the amusement of the crowd?

No, I had only done what I had to do. And I knew at least one other person could understand how I felt—Phoebus, too, had risked everything to do what he thought was right. Knowing that made me care for him all the more. I hoped he was all right. I knew Quasimodo would take good care of him. Phoebus's wound was not life-threatening. All he needed was to rest quietly.

And so did I. "Come on, Djali," I told the goat. "Let's go find someplace to lie down for a while."

I don't know how long I slept. It was Djali who awoke me. He bleated urgently.

"What is it?" I asked, my voice weary and a little annoyed. "What's the matter now?"

Djali danced on his little hooves, seeming more frantic than ever. Finally, I awoke and realized that something must be really wrong.

"Okay, I'm coming," I said, jumping to my feet. "Lead the way."

When we burst into a cavern in the catacombs, the first thing I saw was a large crowd of gypsies gathered together around the stage where an old gallows sat. There were two men standing beneath the strong wooden beam tied with nooses. I rubbed my eyes, trying to figure out what was going on.

Suddenly, I recognized the two men in the nooses.

"Stop!" I screamed, hustling through the crowd.

Clopin was standing beside the two men. He turned to stare in surprise as Djali and I pushed our way toward him. I knew what had 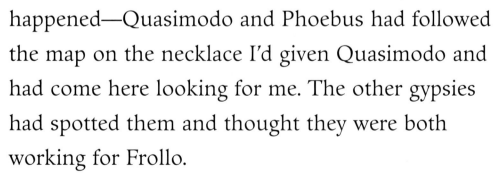 happened—Quasimodo and Phoebus had followed the map on the necklace I'd given Quasimodo and had come here looking for me. The other gypsies had spotted them and thought they were both working for Frollo.

"These men aren't spies!" I cried as I reached the stage. "They're our friends."

Murmurs rose up in the crowd behind me. Clopin shrugged. "Why didn't they say so?" he asked.

I leaped up onto the stage and quickly untied Phoebus and Quasimodo, removing the gags from their mouths.

"We did say so!" they both cried when they could speak.

I quickly explained that Phoebus was the one who had saved the miller's family, while Quasimodo had helped me escape from Notre Dame. Finally, the other gypsies seemed ready to believe me.

Phoebus stepped forward. "We came to warn you," he said. "Frollo's coming. He says he knows where you're hiding, and he's attacking at dawn with a thousand men!"

I gasped along with the others. I had no idea when or how the pair had learned this terrible news, but I didn't doubt them for a second. If Phoebus and Quasimodo, my two trusted friends, said Frollo was coming, I believed them.

"Let's waste no time. We must leave immediately!" I cried.

There was a flurry of activity as everyone scattered, gathering up their few belongings and waking the children. Meanwhile, I turned to Phoebus. Despite everything else, I was happy to see him.

"You took a terrible risk coming here," I said. "It may not exactly show, but we're grateful."

Phoebus smiled, then glanced at his companion. "Don't thank me—thank Quasimodo," he said. "Without his help, I would never have found my way here."

"Nor would I," a voice said from behind.

The voice that spoke those last words sent a chill down my spine. It was Frollo! He was standing in the doorway with a troop of soldiers.

The soldiers raced in. Gypsies screamed and ran for their lives. I looked around desperately for an escape, but there was none. We were surrounded!

CAPTURED

"After twenty years of searching," Frollo exclaimed, "the Court of Miracles is mine at last!" He smirked at Quasimodo. "Dear Quasimodo, I always knew you would someday be of use to me," he said sarcastically.

The bell ringer recoiled in horror. "No!"

I couldn't believe my ears. "What are you talking about, Frollo?" I demanded.

"Why, he led me right to you, my dear," Frollo said.

"You're a liar," I retorted. I knew there was no

way Quasimodo would have betrayed me by bringing Frollo to the Court of Miracles.

Frollo must have followed Quasimodo, unbeknownst to the bell ringer. He betrayed his own ward—using him to find us. And now he had us right where he wanted us. All around me, I saw soldiers taking gypsies prisoner.

Then Frollo stepped toward Phoebus, who was trying to break free from the soldier constraining him. "And look what else I've caught in my net.

Captain Phoebus, back from the dead. Another miracle, no doubt."

"There'll be a little bonfire in the square tomorrow," Frollo announced with obvious glee. "And you're all invited to attend. Lock them up!"

With that, the soldiers dragged us off to prison. They even took away poor Djali.

I spent a miserable night locked in a dank cell with a dozen other gypsies. More of my people were in the adjoining cells. Some of the men talked of escape, but most were silent. We all knew it was useless. This time, there truly seemed to be no way out.

At last, as the night wore on and the others fell silent, I dozed a little. Once, I even began to dream. In my dream, I found a key that opened the cell door. With it, I slipped out and rushed to find Phoebus. I discovered him locked inside his own

cell. Oddly, the cell had no door—only a window blocked by strong iron bars.

Neither of us spoke. I tested the bars with my hands, but even as I did so, I knew the bars would not give. Then Phoebus reached between the bars and took my hands in his own. We stood there for a long moment, still silent, just gazing at each other. . . .

Then I woke up. A sliver of dawn's first light illuminated the cell. All around me, I saw my people huddled together, trying to sleep or just waiting for what was to come.

I could hardly believe it had come to this. Frollo had won—he had stolen our freedom, and soon he would steal our lives.

But I was sure of one thing. He might be able to kill me, but he would never have the satisfaction of seeing me beg for mercy. He would never have my soul.

It wasn't long before soldiers appeared at our cell. They dragged me out alone, leaving the others behind. Leading me outside to the cathedral square, they tied me to a stake. Straw was piled around my feet. Glancing around, I saw that Phoebus along with some of the other gypsies had been brought out and imprisoned in cages nearby.

I also saw that a crowd was gathering. News of the execution must have spread through the city even faster than the flames Frollo's men had started the night before. I was terrified, but I did my best not to let it show.

After a moment, Frollo stepped forward to address the crowd. "The prisoner, Esmeralda, has been found guilty of the crime of witchcraft," he announced. "The sentence—death!"

I heard a few cheers from the crowd, but also a few shouts for my release. But it did no good. The executioner stepped forward, holding a torch. He stared up at me for a moment. Out of the corner of my eye, I saw the Archdeacon step out of the cathedral. But several soldiers blocked his path. He would not be able to save me this time.

Nor would Phoebus. I could see him in his cage, struggling against the iron bars. But just as in my dream, they would not budge.

Frollo stepped forward. He took the torch from

the executioner's hand. I guessed that he wanted to do the deed himself.

"The time has come, gypsy," he said to me. "You stand upon the brink of the abyss." He took a step closer and lowered his voice. "Yet even now it is not too late."

I stared at him. What did he mean by that?

"I can save you from the flames of this world and the next," he went on quietly, his eyes glittering as much as the flame of his torch. "Choose me—or the fire."

Suddenly, I realized what he was offering. If I were to become his slave, he would release me.

There was only one response. I spit in his face.

That brought gasps from the crowd. Frollo looked furious as he wiped away the spittle. When he spoke again, his voice was much more harsh.

"This evil witch has put the soul of every citizen in Paris in mortal jeopardy!" he cried. With that, he lowered the torch and set the kindling at my feet ablaze.

There were cries and murmurs from the crowd. I could already feel the heat around my bare feet as more and more of the kindling caught flame.

For a moment, the only sounds I could hear were the crackling of the fire and the pounding of my own heart. The smoke rose up around me, choking me and making it hard to breathe. Suddenly, I heard a cry:

"Noooooooo!"

Looking up with one last bit of energy, I gasped in surprise. Quasimodo was swinging down toward me on a rope! A moment later, he leaped onto the platform where I was tied. With a quick jerk, he pulled the ropes loose, freeing me.

I was barely conscious by then, and sank against him as he lifted me onto his shoulder. Soldiers were running toward us, but Quasimodo grabbed a burning plank and swung it at them menacingly.

That was the last thing I remembered before I slipped into darkness.

TRUE HEROES

I swam back to consciousness—and almost immediately wished that I hadn't. Breathing was difficult, and every part of my body hurt. My legs ached and my head was pounding.

But I forced myself to open my eyes. I was in the bell tower. Quasimodo was nearby, but he was not looking at me. He was glaring at Frollo, who stood facing him.

Later, I would learn that Quasimodo had carried me to the steps of Notre Dame. Crying out for sanctuary, he had brought me inside.

But that hadn't stopped Frollo. Ordering his soldiers to seize the cathedral, he had smashed his way inside and followed Quasimodo, ignoring the protests of the Archdeacon. He had followed us all the way up to Quasimodo's bell tower. It is possible Frollo didn't realize that, all around him, the people of Paris were rebelling against him, freeing the other prisoners and fighting the soldiers. Or maybe he was too consumed with his own rage to care.

In any case, at the moment my eyes opened, I knew that Frollo was there.

"Quasimodo!" I gasped.

"Esmeralda!" he exclaimed.

As I pushed myself up into a sitting position, Quasimodo turned and hurried toward me. He looked amazed to see me awake.

Frollo seemed much less happy about it. "She lives," he said. Then he drew his sword.

Quasimodo grabbed me, lifting me in his arms as if I weighed no more than a feather. "No!" he shouted at Frollo. Turning, he raced out of the room with me. We burst out onto a balcony.

A moment later, Frollo followed. "Leaving so soon?" he said with a snicker.

Quasimodo climbed down the parapet. I clung to him for dear life. Frollo was still after us—he was trying to reach Quasimodo's hands and wrists with his sword so that the bell ringer would lose his grip and we would fall.

But Quasimodo knew the walls, gargoyles, and parapets better than Frollo could ever imagine. He swung nimbly off the wall onto a nearby section of roof.

Still, Frollo didn't give up. As Quasimodo lowered

us onto a large gargoyle, the judge swung at us with his sword.

"I should have known you'd risk your life to save that gypsy," he told Quasimodo coldly. "Just as your own mother died, trying to save you!"

"What?" Quasimodo gasped. Quasimodo had later told me that for twenty years he believed he had been abandoned, when the truth was much worse. Frollo had killed Quasimodo's mother even as she had tried to gain sanctuary in the cathedral!

While Quasimodo stood there, stunned by this news, Frollo tossed his cloak over Quasimodo. Quasimodo lost his balance and began to fall. But he managed to grab the end of Frollo's cloak and pull. Now it was Frollo who lost his balance and fell. Soon, Frollo dangled over the edge of the roof, clinging to his cloak for dear life.

Quasimodo held onto the end of the cloak with one arm, while clinging to the gargoyle with the other. They hung there for a moment. Fearing that Quasimodo would lose his grip, I reached down and grabbed his arm, trying to keep him from slipping.

"Hold on!" I cried.

But Frollo had managed to crawl up onto a nearby gargoyle. He was still holding his sword. As I clung to Quasimodo, Frollo chuckled as he raised the sword over me.

But at that moment, the gargoyle beneath his feet started to crack. Frollo let out a yell, scrambling for another foothold.

But it was too late! The gargoyle broke off,

sending the evil judge plummeting down, down, down to the square far below.

I hardly noticed—I was too busy trying to hold onto Quasimodo's hands. But he was just too heavy. My weak arms were no match for his weight. His hands started to slip out of mine. Quasimodo was going to fall!

At that moment, two strong arms reached out from a nearby balcony. It was Phoebus! He grabbed Quasimodo just in time, pulling him up over the edge of the balcony to safety.

We all hugged each other gratefully. I could hardly believe that the nightmare was over. Frollo was dead, and we were safe!

I gazed up at Phoebus's face. Just a short while earlier, I had been sure I would never look upon it again in this world.

As we smiled at each other, I felt Quasimodo take my hand. He took Phoebus's as well. Then he joined them together. As he stepped away, Phoebus and I kissed.

A few minutes later, the three of us walked across the nave of the deserted cathedral. The light that filtered through the stained-glass windows created a golden glow on the marble floor.

The townspeople who had gathered in the square cheered when they saw us step into the doorway. We smiled at them gratefully. They were as happy about their freedom from Frollo's evil rule as we were. Best of all, they were all hailing Quasimodo as a hero.

I could tell that Quasimodo was a little nervous about all the attention. That wasn't surprising, considering what had happened the last time a crowd had cheered for him!

But this time, it would be different. As we stood there, a little girl broke away from the crowd and came forward. She stepped toward Quasimodo. For

a moment she seemed nervous, staring up at his misshapen features.

Then she dashed forward and wrapped her arms around him. Quasimodo smiled with wonder, leaning down to accept the little girl's embrace.

I smiled at Phoebus. At last, our friend would have his chance to live a good life outside the cathedral doors.

We stepped forward as the bells of Notre Dame

rang out above us. Moments later in the crowded square, I spotted a familiar, furry little face.

"Djali!" I cried, reaching out as the goat leaped toward me happily. I was so relieved that he was safe!

Then I danced through the celebrating crowd, greeting old friends and new ones alike. Everyone was filled with joy.

Still, I was glad when Phoebus found me a few minutes later and pulled me into a quiet corner. He put his arm around me, took my hand, and smiled down at me.

"Well, what do you think?" he asked.

I wasn't sure what he meant. "What do I think of what?"

"Of this. All this," he replied, waving a hand to indicate the crowds still celebrating nearby. "I mean, Quasimodo is a hero, your people are safe, Frollo is

gone forever, and the
battle is over. And
most important of
all, we can finally
be together."

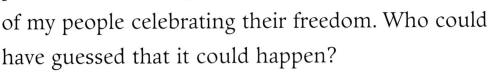

I glanced out
at the crowds of
happy, faces. It made
my heart swell with
pride to see so many
of my people celebrating their freedom. Who could
have guessed that it could happen?

They say that Paris is the most modern of cities,
full of modern people with modern ideas. Perhaps
now, finally, we gypsies could be a part of it. Perhaps
now we could step out of the shadows and be proud
of who we were, just like my friend Quasimodo.